Malory Towers

Enid Blyton™

Enid Blyton™

Secrets AT Malory Towers

Written by Pamela Cox

EGMONT

EGMONT

We bring stories to life

Secrets at Malory Towers first published in Great Britain 2009
by Egmont UK Limited
239 Kensington High Street
London W8 6SA

ISBN 978 1 4052 4476 3

5 7 9 10 8 6 4

A CIP catalogue record for this title is available from the British Library

Typeset by Avon DataSet Ltd, Bidford on Avon, Warwickshire
Printed and bound in Great Britain by the CPI Group

Contents

On the train

'Well, Felicity,' said Susan Blake. 'How does it feel to be going back to Malory Towers as Head Girl?'

Head Girl! No matter how often she heard the words, Felicity Rivers still felt a little thrill of pleasure at them.

She had been astonished, disbelieving, delighted and – above all – honoured, when Miss Grayling, the Head mistress of Malory Towers, had announced at the end of last term that she was to be Head Girl. And Susan had felt exactly the same when the Head had told her that she was to be Felicity's deputy, assisting her friend with her duties. The two girls had been best friends since they were first formers, and were very close indeed. Miss Grayling knew that they would make an excellent team, for both girls were responsible, trustworthy and kind-hearted. She could certainly rely on them to do their best for Malory Towers and its pupils.

Of course, Felicity's parents had been proud and delighted too, and so had her sister Darrell, who had once been Head Girl of Malory Towers herself. Darrell had hugged her younger sister excitedly when Felicity arrived home for the holidays, crying, 'Congratulations! Miss Grayling has made a splendid choice. I wonder if you feel as thrilled as I did when she told me that I was to be Head Girl?'

'I should rather think I do!' laughed Felicity, hugging Darrell back. 'Thrilled and overwhelmed, for it is a tremendous responsibility.'

'I'm sure that you will do a splendid job,' the girls' father had said, overhearing this. 'Just as Darrell did, when she was Head Girl.'

'And you will have Susan to back you up,' Mrs Rivers had added. 'My goodness, it's becoming quite a family tradition, isn't it? Perhaps one day, my dears, your daughters will be Head Girls of Malory Towers too.'

This was a very pleasant thought indeed, and Felicity had beamed at her parents and sister, seeing the love and pride in their faces and feeling a warm glow inside. It was a feeling that had lasted all through the holidays and still lingered.

'It's going to be a very testing term for both of us,' said Felicity now. 'What with our new responsibilities *and* studying for Higher Cert.'

The two girls were sitting in the little café at the railway station, waiting for the train that was to take them back to Malory Towers, and Susan gave a groan, saying, 'Higher Cert! That's the only thing that has spoiled what has been an otherwise marvellous holiday for me – having to spend some time studying.'

'Well, it will all be worth it when we pass,' said Felicity sensibly. 'Though in some ways I can't help envying those who aren't going in for it, for they will have a nice, carefree term, while the rest of us are slaving away like mad.'

'Yes,' said Susan with a rueful grin. 'Sometimes it pays to be a duffer! Nora and Delia aren't going in for it, and nor is Amy.'

'Bonnie is, though,' said Felicity with a grin. 'She didn't intend to, then June said that she thought Bonnie was very wise, for she would never pass in a million years.'

'And, of course, Bonnie saw that as a challenge, and at once changed her mind,' laughed Susan. 'Jolly clever of June, for Bonnie has a good brain, if she chooses to use it.'

'Well, June is the one person in our form who won't have to worry about studying,' said Felicity rather enviously. 'She only has to read a page once to memorise it. Darrell says that her cousin, Alicia, was exactly the same.'

'Yes, it's so unfair,' said Susan. 'June will get top marks without even trying, while the rest of us will be burning the midnight oil and worrying whether we will manage to scrape through.'

'June won't get off completely scot-free, though,' said Felicity. 'She is still games captain, and will have to work hard at that.'

Just then the door of the little café opened, and a girl wearing the Malory Towers uniform entered.

She was thin, and rather plain, with straight, mousy-brown hair, and her eyes looked very scared behind the big glasses she wore.

Felicity and Susan guessed that she must be a new girl, and felt rather sorry for her, as she looked so nervous. As Head Girl, it was Felicity's duty to make her feel at ease, so she called out, 'Hallo there! You must be waiting for the train to Malory Towers.'

The girl looked at Felicity, then at Susan, her expression becoming even more scared, then she advanced rather timidly, and said in a very quiet voice, 'That's right. I'm starting in the sixth form.'

'Well, we are in the sixth form too,' said Susan. 'Do sit down and join us. This is Felicity Rivers, Head Girl of Malory Towers, and I am Susan Blake, her best friend and deputy.'

This information seemed to startle the girl a little, for she blinked rapidly, before sitting down and saying, 'I'm Alice Johnson. My goodness, what luck to bump into the two most important girls in the school.'

'Well, I don't know that I would go that far,' laughed Felicity. 'Miss Grayling, our Head mistress, would most certainly say that each girl at Malory Towers is as important as the next, and she is quite right.'

'And a lot of the lower school would argue that our fellow sixth former, June, is the most important person in the school,' said Susan. 'She is games captain, you see, and most of the youngsters simply adore her.'

Alice smiled rather nervously at this, and, quite suddenly, it struck Felicity that there was something oddly familiar about her. Then the smile disappeared, and so did Felicity's feeling that she had seen the girl somewhere before. It really was most strange!

Susan glanced at the big clock that hung on the wall, saying, 'I would offer you a cup of tea, Alice, but the train will be here any minute. We really should go.'

So the three girls left the café, weaving their way through groups of Malory Towers girls, mistresses and parents, until they reached the platform from which their train would leave.

Miss Potts, the house-mistress of North Tower, was there, with a small group of excited, chattering first formers, and she greeted Felicity and Susan with a smile.

'Well, girls,' she said. 'It is nice to see you back. I never got the opportunity at the end of last term to congratulate you both. Felicity, I am sure that you will make a fine Head Girl, and Susan, I know that you will do everything that you can to help.'

The two girls thanked Miss Potts, and, nodding towards the unruly first formers, Felicity said, 'It seems strange to think that one of these youngsters will one day be Head Girl.'

'At the moment, it seems quite impossible to believe!' said Miss Potts drily. 'Daphne, *is* there any need to yell like that? Katie is standing right next to you and she isn't deaf, though she may well end up that way if you keep shouting in her ear like that.'

'Sorry, Miss Potts,' said Daphne, a slim, pretty girl with short dark curls and merry brown eyes.

'Why, it's Daffy Hope!' said Felicity. 'Hello, Daffy. Sally told me that you were starting at Malory Towers this term, and asked me to look out for you.'

'Is that Sally's young sister?' asked Susan as she, Felicity and Alice boarded the train. 'She seems a bit of a handful.'

'Oh no, I've met her heaps of times and she's a very nice, well-behaved kid,' said Felicity. 'I daresay she's just excited at going off to boarding school for the first time.'

Sally Hope was Darrell's best friend, and the two families had become very close over the years, so when Sally had asked Felicity to keep an eye on her young sister, she had agreed at once. It wouldn't be a very difficult task, she thought, for Daphne – or Daffy, as most people called her – was such a good kid, and not the kind of girl to get into mischief.

The three sixth formers quickly found an empty carriage, and, as they took their seats, Susan looked out of the window and said, 'I can see June and Freddie coming along the platform. We must save a couple of seats for them.'

But June and Freddie did not get on the train immediately, for they were distracted by a little by-play on the platform. While the two girls stopped to greet Miss Potts, a latecomer arrived, accompanied by her mother, and it soon became evident that she wasn't in the best of moods.

'I don't see why the chauffeur couldn't have driven me to school,' she complained loudly. 'It's simply beastly having to rough it on the train.'

'Now, Violet dear,' said her mother rather nervously.

'You know very well that Benson had to drive Daddy to an important meeting today.'

'He could quite easily have taken a taxi,' said Violet, looking sullen. 'Then I shouldn't have had to get up so early. You know how I hate getting up early, Mummy.'

'Yes, darling, but you know that you will have to get used to it when you are at school,' her mother said. 'You will get into awful trouble if you sleep in and are late for breakfast, you know.'

'It's too bad!' said Violet, looking as if she were about to burst into tears. 'There will be all sorts of beastly rules that I shall have to keep, and I shan't be able to have my own way at all.'

And Violet was used to getting her own way, thought June, watching the little scene in amusement. A little *too* used to it, by the look of things.

Violet was a short, plump girl, with carefully curled golden hair, rather small grey eyes and a turned-up nose.

'As though she has a bad smell under it,' murmured Daffy Hope to the little group of first formers, giving a sniff and imitating Violet's high and mighty expression.

The first formers giggled at this, and June, overhearing, had to hide a grin as she glanced at Daffy. She didn't know who this cheeky little first former was, but she had certainly hit the nail on the head!

The spoilt Violet, meanwhile, was just complaining to her mother about how ugly the school uniform was, and as she stamped her foot angrily, Miss Potts decided to take a hand in the matter.

'Good morning,' she said, going across and holding out her hand to Violet's mother. 'You must be Mrs Forsyth, and this, I presume, is Violet. I am Miss Potts, house-mistress of North Tower.'

Mrs Forsyth shook Miss Potts's hand and said, 'I'm pleased to meet you, Miss Potts. I'm afraid that Violet is feeling a little under the weather today. You see, she has always had a governess before, and has never been to school. You must understand that she is rather nervous.'

Miss Potts had met Violet's type before, and quickly sized her up as a spoilt mother's girl. The child wasn't nervous at all, merely furious that she was being sent away to school, where she would have to do as the others did, and wouldn't be able to get her own way by throwing tantrums. Well, perhaps Malory Towers would do her good, and Violet would learn to settle down and be sensible. Miss Potts, glancing round at the other first formers, who were looking at Violet with a mixture of contempt and amusement, certainly hoped so, or things would be very difficult for the girl.

The mistress had also sized up Mrs Forsyth – a pleasant enough woman, but rather weak and silly. Her lips were beginning to tremble now, and Miss Potts knew that, if she was not firm, there would be a long and emotional farewell, which would not do either Violet or her mother any good at all.

So she laid a firm hand on Violet's shoulder and said briskly, 'Come along then, Violet. Say goodbye to your mother quickly, please, then pick up your night case and get on the train.'

Both Violet and her mother looked rather affronted at being robbed of their dramatic farewell, but neither of them dared flout the stern Miss Potts, so they had to content themselves with a brief hug and promises to write.

Then the first formers, along with June and Freddie, moved towards the train, Daffy Hope managing to position herself behind Violet, and sticking her tongue out behind her back.

Once again, June's lips twitched. What a naughty little monkey that girl was, yet there was something rather likeable about her.

Violet, however, thought differently, for she turned round just in time to see Daffy with her tongue out, and scowled at her. Before she could say anything to Daffy, though, June said firmly, 'Get on the train at once, please. You're holding everyone up.'

Violet turned her scowl on June, but one look at the sixth former's face warned her that it would be most unwise to argue! Quickly lowering her eyes from June's, Violet turned away and clambered aboard the train.

Miss Potts remained on the platform, waiting for any stragglers, while June and Freddie, joining the other three sixth formers, were greeted warmly.

The two newcomers looked at Alice curiously, and Felicity said, 'This is Alice Johnson, our new girl. Alice, this is June, our school games captain, and her friend, Freddie Holmes.'

Alice gave her nervous smile, and greeted the two girls in her quiet voice, while June's sharp eyes narrowed.

'Have I met you somewhere before?' she asked.

'Oh, no,' said Alice, shaking her head. 'We have never met before.'

'That's odd,' said June. 'For there's something familiar about you. Perhaps you remind me of someone, though I can't for the life of me think who it is at the moment. Never mind, I'm sure it will come to me.'

Alice looked quite terrified at this thought, and Felicity said, 'That's funny, because earlier on I thought that I recognised you too, though I'm quite sure we have never met. Have you ever had a sister at Malory Towers?'

'No, I'm an only child,' answered Alice.

She had turned rather red, and Freddie, guessing that the girl didn't like being the centre of attention, quickly changed the subject and began telling the girls about Violet Forsyth.

'My goodness, she sounds a perfect little beast,' said Susan.

'Well, Miss Potts won't stand any nonsense from her,' said Felicity.

'I don't think the first-form kids will, either,' said June with a smile. 'One of them in particular seems an imp, and she soon let Violet know what she thought of her. I don't know the kid's name, but she was a pretty little thing – dark, curly hair and laughing brown eyes.'

'Why, that sounds like Daffy Hope,' said Felicity. 'Sally's sister.'

'Really?' said June, raising her dark brows in surprise and saying rather mockingly, 'I would never have guessed, for she is the opposite of solid, sensible Sally.'

'Nonsense,' said Felicity. 'I can't think why you believe that she's an imp, June. And Susan, you said that she looked like a handful, but you're both quite wrong, for she is every bit as sensible and responsible as Sally.'

'Is she?' said June, with a quizzical look at Felicity. 'Or are you sure that *you* aren't mistaken, Felicity?'

In the first-form carriage, meanwhile, Daffy Hope was quickly establishing herself as leader of the first form, the others liking her mischievous nature and sense of fun. For June and Susan were quite right. There were two sides to Daffy Hope. The sweet, well-behaved girl that her family was so proud of was very different from the Daffy her school friends knew.

Indeed, Mrs Hope had been most upset when the form mistress at Daffy's prep school had spoken to her about the girl's naughty behaviour.

Daffy had talked her way out of it easily, convincing her mother that the mistress had got her confused with another girl called Daphne, and for the rest of the term she had not dared misbehave. But now that she was away from home, and her parents, it was quite another matter.

Daffy was at a slight advantage to the others, for while they were alone, and feeling rather shy and nervous, she had her best friend from prep school with her.

Katie was Daffy's partner in mischief, and ably seconded her friend as she kept the first form in stitches.

One person who was not impressed with Daffy, however, was Violet. The only thing that had made her agree to come to school was the thought that she would be able to lord it over the others. She had pictured them vying for her friendship, but instead they were all over that silly Daffy. It simply wouldn't do!

So Violet raised her voice, and said to the carriage at large, 'It was my birthday last week.'

No one quite knew what to say to this, so there was an awkward silence, then the girl went on, 'Mummy and Daddy bought me a kitten, for a present. But it's not just an ordinary kitten, you know, it's a pedigree Siamese, and worth an absolute fortune. It would make you stare if I told you how much Daddy had paid for it.'

The girls *were* staring – in disbelief. But Violet decided that their silence meant that they were very impressed indeed, and went on boastfully, 'She sleeps in her own special bed, lined with velvet, you know, and has her own toys, and she is fed on chicken and fish, not shop-bought cat food, like ordinary cats. Her name is Princess Willow, but I just call her Willow, for short.'

'Why not call her Princess, instead?' asked one of the first formers, Maggie, who felt a little uncomfortable that no one was responding to Violet.

'Oh, it's so silly,' said Violet, putting her hand up to her mouth and giving a little giggle. 'You see, Princess is Daddy's nickname for me. So we couldn't give my kitten the same name.'

'What a lovely nickname,' said Daffy very sweetly.

'You know, Violet, I think we should give you a nickname too. Don't you agree, girls?'

The others, ready to agree to anything Daffy said, nodded eagerly, while Violet smiled at this. She had read several school stories, and knew that only the most popular girls were given nicknames. She really *had* made a good impression.

Daffy smiled at her, and said, 'Yes, I've come up with a very good nickname for you, Violet. Your Highness!'

'Oh!' said Violet, rather surprised at this odd choice of nickname. 'Is that because you think I look like a princess?'

'No,' answered Daffy. 'It's because you're *high* and mighty, you're always on your *high* horse and you've always got your nose stuck *high* in the air!'

The others roared, while Violet turned red with rage, and gave an infuriated squeal. 'Even her voice is high!' laughed Katie.

Violet simmered with rage. How dare that horrid Daffy make fun of her? Oh, she was going to hate it at Malory Towers, she just knew it, with no one to spoil her and pet her, or take her side against these beastly girls. If only she could persuade her parents to take her away!

Back at Malory Towers

It was a very long journey to Malory Towers, but most of the older girls were used to this, and had brought books with them to while away the time if the conversation flagged. The youngsters, however, hadn't, so they soon became either very bored and restless, or very tired, and fell asleep.

In the sixth-form carriage, only Alice had fallen asleep, while Felicity and Susan read their books, and June and Freddie pored over a crossword puzzle together.

Looking up from her book, Susan happened to glance across at the sleeping Alice, whose glasses had slid sideways across her face, giving her rather a comical look. Susan smiled, then she stared harder at Alice, and whispered, 'You're right!'

'Who's right?' said June. 'And, more importantly, what is she right about?'

'Alice,' answered Susan, leaning forward and keeping her voice low, so as not to disturb the sleeping girl. 'You and Felicity said that she looked familiar, and I couldn't see it myself, but now I do.'

Alice suddenly shifted position, so that her hair fell over her face, and Freddie said, 'Blow! I wanted to have a good look, though I really can't say that I recognised her on first sight.'

'She seems awfully nervous and timid,' whispered Susan.

'Yes, but she's pleasant enough,' said Felicity. 'I expect that Alice will open up a bit when she knows us better.'

'I wonder if she's any good at lacrosse?' said June, ever the games captain. 'I doubt it somehow. She doesn't look the sporting type.'

Just then Alice stirred, stretched and sat up, blinking as she pushed her glasses back on to her nose.

The others immediately felt guilty, and hoped that she hadn't overheard them talking about her, although they hadn't said anything bad.

But it seemed that Alice hadn't heard a thing, for she said in her soft voice, 'Oh dear! Did I fall asleep? How rude of me.'

'Don't give it a thought,' said June airily. 'We old hands usually bring something to keep us occupied on the journey, so that we don't drop off.'

'Well, I shall remember that next term,' said Alice.

'At least the worst of the journey is over now,' said Felicity. 'We shall be at the station very soon, then we go the rest of the way by coach.'

The first formers were all wide awake when the train stopped at the station, and thoroughly over-excited. But Miss Potts had joined them now, and Daffy Hope, realising that she was a force to be reckoned with, was on her best behaviour, she and Katie walking sedately beside the mistress as they made their way to the big coaches.

Felicity spotted her, noting her sweet expression, and the respectful way in which she looked up at Miss Potts when the mistress addressed her. How on earth could Susan and June, both of them normally so shrewd, have misread her character so badly?

She might have changed her opinion had she been on the same coach as the first formers, and seen Daffy pulling faces behind Miss Potts's back, and making the others laugh by pushing the tip of her nose up to imitate Violet's snooty expression each time the girl looked at her.

But the sixth formers were on a different coach, so Felicity remained in blissful ignorance.

Alice seemed very interested as the others pointed out various landmarks to her on the way to Malory Towers, her eyes lighting up as she saw the sea in the distance.

'We aren't allowed to swim in it, though,' Felicity warned her. 'There was a terrible accident a few years ago, when one of the old sixth formers tried swimming in the sea. The current caught her and pulled her on to some rocks, and she was badly hurt. It was only thanks to June that she didn't drown. So stick to the school swimming-pool, if you fancy a dip. It's quite beautiful, you know, for it's hollowed out of rocks and filled by the sea.'

'Yes, I remember,' said Alice, and Felicity stared at her. How on earth could Alice remember the swimming-pool, when she had never been to Malory Towers – unless she was lying?

At once the girl turned red, and said hastily, 'I mean, I

remember my mother telling me about the pool. She saw it, you see, when she came down to see Miss Grayling about me coming here.'

Well, that was perfectly possible, thought Felicity, for Miss Grayling often showed parents who were thinking of sending their girls to Malory Towers around the school, and she always took them to the swimming-pool. And Alice was certainly very nervous and timid, which explained why her manner was rather strange sometimes. So Felicity dismissed her doubts, and turned her attention instead to the first glimpse of Malory Towers, which thrilled her just as much now as it had when she was a first former.

Alice gave a gasp as she saw the beautiful old building perched on the cliff-top. Each of its four towers – North, South, East and West – was a separate house, with its own dormitories, dining-room and common-rooms.

'Impressive, isn't it?' said June, smiling at Alice's look of wonder.

'I'll say,' breathed Alice. 'I feel so lucky to be here.'

Moments later, the coaches drew to a stop at the top of the long driveway, and the girls retrieved their night cases from the luggage rack, before getting out.

As always on the first day of term, the grounds were very busy indeed, as girls greeted one another noisily and said goodbye to parents.

June's sharp eyes spotted some of their fellow sixth formers, and she said, 'Let's go and say hallo. Come along, Alice.'

Alice followed meekly in the wake of the others as they made their way across the lawn, and soon she was being introduced to yet more sixth formers. There was the calm, good-tempered Pam and her scatterbrained friend Nora, and the rather snobbish Amy, with her little friend Bonnie.

All four girls greeted Alice, and Pam said, 'Let's go and give our health certificates in to Matron. Got yours, Alice?'

The girl nodded, and the sixth formers made their way towards North Tower. They passed several younger girls on the way, and Felicity was amused, and rather touched, to hear the awe in their voices as they greeted her.

Correctly reading her expression, June clapped her on the back and said, 'You'll have to get used to it, you know, now that you are Head Girl. The younger ones are bound to look up to you no end.'

'Of course, you've already had experience of it, haven't you?' said Felicity, for June had been games captain of the school since she was in the fifth form. 'I don't know that I shall *ever* get used to it, though.'

Matron greeted the sixth formers with a cheery smile, and said, 'Well, well, it seems hard to believe that you are all top formers now. And fancy you being Head Girl, Felicity! Why, I can remember you coming in here as a shy, rather scared first former. And you too, Susan.'

'What about me, Matron?' asked June.

'You were never shy and scared in your life, June!' laughed Matron. 'But I remember you, all right. Now, let me have your health certificates, then I will allocate you your studies.'

The girls listened to this with mingled excitement and sadness.

It would be marvellous to have their own studies, of course, but they would miss the happy times they had shared together in their big common-room.

As Matron handed out study keys, Felicity noticed that Alice was looking rather forlorn, and realised that it was going to be especially hard on the new girl having a study to herself. It would have been much easier for her to get to know the others if they had had a common-room. The sixth formers would have to coax her out of her shell a little, decided Felicity, then she would feel quite comfortable about popping into the others' studies whenever she felt like a chat.

So Felicity was pleased when Matron said, 'Felicity, as Alice is the new girl, I have given her the study next door to yours, then you are on hand if she feels a bit lost and lonely.'

'Good idea, Matron,' said Felicity, giving the new girl's arm a friendly squeeze. 'Don't worry, Alice, if you need some company in the evenings you can always pop into my study. I'm sure that goes for the others too.'

Everyone agreed at once, though Amy was rather half-hearted. She always chose her friends very carefully indeed, and didn't think that she would have anything in common with this rather plain, dull girl.

The sixth formers were simply dying to see their

studies, and unpacked as quickly as possible. There were four more sixth formers in the dormitory, already putting their things away, when the girls arrived – Gillian, Delia, Julie and Lucy, and the others greeted them happily.

'Hallo! Had good hols?'

'Have you been to Matron yet and got your study keys?'

'My word, Gillian, just look at all your freckles! You must have spent all summer out in the sun.'

'Julie, I suppose you've brought Jack with you, as usual. And Lucy, how is Sandy?'

Julie and Lucy were both horse-mad, and brought their horses, Jack and Sandy, to school with them each term. The two girls were great friends, and, over the years, their horses had become great friends too, Lucy swearing that Sandy pined during the holidays when he couldn't be with Jack.

'Do hurry up and unpack, everyone,' said Gillian, who was busy tying back her mane of auburn hair. 'We're simply dying to see our studies. Matron has put Delia and I next to one another, so we are both very pleased.'

Felicity looked at Gillian's friend Delia, who was beaming all over her face, and thought how much the girl had changed since starting at Malory Towers.

Delia had been rather diffident and lacking in confidence as a new girl, but then, almost by accident, she had discovered that she possessed a wonderful talent for singing and writing songs. That, along with the friendship she had forged with Gillian, had done wonders for her confidence, and Delia had blossomed. She was still – as she said herself – a complete duffer at lessons, and would never be top of the class, but she was a pleasant, kind-hearted girl, popular with everyone.

The sixth-form studies were on the floor below the dormitory, and each girl opened the door of her own little room with a feeling of anticipation. They were furnished with a desk and chair, as well as a comfortable armchair, and had a bookcase on which the girls could put personal belongings, such as photographs, as well as their books.

Felicity wasted no time in getting out a framed photograph of her parents and sister, Darrell, but instead of placing it on a shelf, she put it on her desk, so that she would be able to see it every time she looked up from her work.

There was a great deal of to-ing and fro-ing as the girls went up and downstairs to fetch things to make their studies look more 'homely', as Nora put it. Then, of course, they had to visit everyone else's rooms and give their opinions.

'I say, Felicity's is bigger than ours, and she has *two* armchairs. Most unfair!'

'Well, the Head Girl always gets the biggest study.'

'Ours are much cosier, anyway, though I can't say I'm awfully keen on the curtains in mine.'

Most of the girls had added a photograph of their parents, or a beloved pet, or some other little touch to show who the study belonged to. Bonnie had spent the holidays embroidering a beautiful cushion, which she had placed proudly on the armchair. And Nora's mother had given her a little vase, while Susan's had donated a small table-lamp.

But one little study remained curiously bereft of all personal belongings, and that was Alice's.

'Haven't you brought a photograph of your family?' asked Pam.

'I meant to, but I must have forgotten to pack it,' said the girl rather dolefully. 'I must say, my poor little study looks awfully plain next to yours. I shall have to write to Mother and get her to send me something to brighten it up.'

'If you like, Alice, I can make you a cushion,' offered Bonnie, taking pity on the girl. 'Just like mine, but in different colours.'

Alice's face lit up at this, but before she could accept, June said, 'Oh no, you can't, my girl. Not if you're studying for Higher Cert. You'll have no time for sewing or embroidery.'

Bonnie's face fell, and June went on wickedly, 'Unless, of course, you've changed your mind and decided that it's too much like hard work.'

'Nothing of the sort!' declared Bonnie, a firm set to her delicate little chin. 'I'm going in for Higher Cert, all right, and I jolly well intend to pass with flying colours!'

'That's the spirit, Bonnie!' said Lucy, patting the girl on the back.

'Oh well, it looks as if you'll have to send for something from home after all, Alice,' said Delia.

'I shall make you a cushion once the exams are over, Alice,' said Bonnie. 'That's a promise.'

Just then the bell went for tea, which everyone was very glad of, for they were all extremely hungry.

As they made their way down to the big dining-room, the sixth formers were overtaken by a noisy horde of first formers, Daffy Hope among them, and Felicity called out, 'Less noise, please, kids! I know you're all excited, but do try to calm down a little.'

'Sorry, Felicity,' said Daffy, at her most demure, and Felicity grinned to herself as the youngsters went on their way, slightly more quietly. Little monkeys! Even sweet, angelic Daffy was getting caught up in the first-day excitement. And who could blame her, for surely there wasn't a better place to be than Malory Towers.

3

Who is Alice?

After breakfast the following morning, all of the new girls had to go and see Miss Grayling, the Head mistress.

Almost all of the first formers were new, and there were quite a lot of them, so they went in first. Then it was the turn of the other new girls, including Alice. As Head Girl, Felicity escorted them all to the Head's room, then she sat outside on a chair, waiting for Alice, so that she could show her the way to the sixth-form classroom.

Miss Grayling was a serene, calm-faced woman, with startlingly blue eyes, which could look very cold when she was angry, or twinkle brightly if she was amused. She was also extremely shrewd, and had an extraordinary ability to read the characters of the girls who stood before her. As she addressed each girl, asking her name and her form, her eyes seemed to linger on Alice, for she knew a great deal about the girl. The sixth formers would have been very surprised indeed if they had known all that Miss Grayling knew!

Then Miss Grayling gave the little speech that she always made at the beginning of each term, and Alice listened intently, taking in every word. Really, she felt as if the Head might have been speaking to her, and her alone!

'One day,' began Miss Grayling, 'you will leave Malory Towers and go out into the world as young women. You should take with you eager minds, kind hearts and a will to help. You should take with you a good understanding of many things, and a willingness to accept responsibility, and show yourselves as women to be loved and trusted.'

The Head paused for a moment, her eyes moving from one girl to the other, then she went on in her low, clear voice, 'All of these things you are able to learn at Malory Towers – if you *will*. I do not count as our successes those who have won scholarships, or passed exams, though these are good things to do. I count as our successes those who learn to be good-hearted and kind, sensible and trustworthy, good, sound women the world can lean on. Our failures are those who do not learn those things in the time they are here.'

Again Miss Grayling paused, and Alice vowed there and then that she was going to be a success, whatever it took.

The Head spoke again, saying, 'Some of you will find it easy to learn these things, others will find it hard. But they must be learned, one way or the other, if you are to be happy after you have left here, and if you are to bring happiness to others.'

She was about to say more, but suddenly the telephone on her desk rang.

'I think that this is an important telephone call that I

have been expecting,' said Miss Grayling. 'You may go to your class-rooms, girls, but please take my words with you, and think about them.'

The Head's clear voice had carried to Felicity, waiting outside. The girl remembered listening to the very same words when she had first come to Malory Towers, and she knew what Miss Grayling had been about to say next – *'You will all get a tremendous lot out of your time at Malory Towers. See that you give a lot back.'*

The words had made a great impression on Felicity, and had stayed with her throughout her time at the school. She hoped that she had succeeded in giving something back to the school that had taught her so much, and would continue to do so in her last year.

The door of Miss Grayling's study opened, and the new girls emerged. One look at their rapt faces was enough to tell Felicity that the Head had made a great impression on them too.

Alice's eyes were shining behind her big glasses, and she said to Felicity in her rather high, nervous voice, 'What a marvellous person Miss Grayling is! I really feel that I want to do my best, for myself and for the school.'

'Well, I'm very pleased to hear it,' said Felicity with a smile. 'We'd better get along to our class-room now, for Miss Oakes will be there soon and she won't appreciate it if we are late.'

'Is that our form-mistress?' asked Alice. 'What is she like?'

'I don't know her very well,' said Felicity. 'But

according to last year's sixth formers she can be rather stern, though she is always fair. And she doesn't have much of a sense of humour, which is a shame.'

Miss Oakes *didn't* have a great sense of humour, but she was a fine teacher and, although she didn't suffer fools gladly, took a keen interest in the welfare of her girls.

There was a low hum of chatter in the sixth-form class-room as the girls waited for their mistress, but no ragging or fooling about. As top formers, that kind of thing was quite beneath the girls' dignity.

In the first-form class-room, however, it was a very different story, and the girls were making a terrific racket as they waited for their mistress, Miss Potts.

The head-girl of the first form was a quiet, rather colourless girl named Faith, and she had been chosen because she had already been at Malory Towers for one term.

'Faith is not a natural leader in any way,' Miss Potts had said to Miss Grayling, when they were discussing who should be head of the first form. 'But it would be quite unfair to make one of the new girls head-girl over her.'

'Very true,' Miss Grayling had agreed. 'Besides, we don't yet know the characters of the new girls, and what qualities they have. So it would be quite impossible to predict which of them might make good head-girls.'

'Quite,' Miss Potts had said. 'And who knows, this might be the making of Faith, and bring out some hidden depths in her.'

So Faith, rather to her alarm, suddenly found herself

27

head-girl of a very unruly first form. But, although Faith might be head-girl, Daffy Hope was emerging as the true leader of the form. Naughty, lively and mischievous, every girl wanted to be her friend, whereas poor Faith was too quiet and shy to be very popular.

Someone who was decidedly *un*popular was Violet, and the first formers had soon grown heartily tired of her conceit, her boasting and her stuck-up ways. Violet had also taken an intense dislike to Daffy. Not only was she extremely jealous of the girl's popularity, but the horrid nickname that Daffy had given her – *Your Highness* – had stuck, and how she hated it!

Daffy was telling an amusing story about something that had happened in the holidays, keeping the others in fits, while Violet watched, her little snub nose in the air and an expression of disdain on her round face.

Katie spotted her, and said, 'What's the matter, Your Highness?'

'I know what it is,' said Daffy, giggling. 'We forgot to curtsey when Violet came into the class-room.'

And, with that, the naughty girl got to her feet and curtsied dantily, while the others roared with laughter, so loudly that they didn't hear Miss Potts approaching.

Violet, turning red, jumped to her feet and began giving Daffy a tremendous scold. Unfortunately for her, however, she had her back to the class-room door, and didn't see the form-mistress come in. But wicked Daffy did, and at once she put on a very hurt, scared expression, saying to Violet in a soft, trembling voice, 'Oh, how cruel and hurtful of you! I can't think what I've done to make you dislike me so.'

Miss Potts, accustomed to the utmost respect from her classes, was not at all pleased. The girls hadn't stood up when she came in, and no one had held the door open for her. Her sharp eyes took in the scene at a glance, looking from Daffy's innocent face to Violet's red, angry one.

'Would someone care to explain to me what is going on here?' she asked, her tone icy.

No one did, a scared hush falling over the first form now, and Miss Potts turned to Faith, saying, 'Well, Faith? The other girls might be new, but you have already been in my form for a term, and know the standard of behaviour I expect. That is why you are head-girl. And, as head-girl, it is your duty to keep the others in order.'

'Sorry, Miss Potts,' mumbled a very red-faced Faith, getting to her feet. The others hastily stood up too, and Daffy, feeling a little sorry for Faith, came to her rescue.

'I'm terribly sorry, Miss Potts,' she said, at her most charming. 'Violet and I were having a – a little disagreement, and that is why we didn't hear you come in. It won't happen again, I promise.'

'I should hope not,' said Miss Potts sternly, looking hard at Daffy. 'You are Daphne Hope, aren't you?'

'Yes, Miss Potts,' answered Daffy. 'My older sister, Sally, was in your form many years ago.'

'Yes, I remember Sally well,' said the mistress, her stern features relaxing a little. Sally had been a model pupil – reliable, hard-working, honest and trustworthy –

and Miss Potts hoped that her younger sister would take after her.

'Well,' she said at last. 'As this is the first full day of term, we will say no more about it. But be warned, all of you, that any further incidents like this will be punished most severely. Now, please sit down.'

The girls did as they were told, but not before Daffy and Violet exchanged angry glares, while Faith looked from one to the other uneasily. Her first day as head-girl, and she was already in hot water with Miss Potts. How on earth was she going to win the respect of her unruly fellow first formers and keep order? Oh dear, it looked as if her first term as head-girl could also be her last!

Things were going much more smoothly for the sixth formers, though those taking Higher Certificate grimaced when they received their timetables, and realised how much extra work they would have to do.

Felicity felt quite envious when she overheard Delia whispering to Nora, 'I say, we have quite a lot of free time each week, as we don't have to study for Higher Cert. I think that I'm going to enjoy this term!'

Alice wasn't studying for Higher Certificate either, and she intended to make good use of her free time by making herself as helpful as she could to the others, as well as to the mistresses. Her brains weren't of the highest order, and she was no good at sports, yet she desperately wanted to become one of Malory Towers' successes. And she meant to do her best to become a good and trustworthy person, the kind of girl who would make Miss Grayling proud.

So, when Miss Oakes asked for a volunteer to hand out books, Alice leapt to her feet so quickly that she almost knocked over her chair.

'I'll do that, Miss Oakes,' she said eagerly.

And another opportunity to be of assistance arose later, when Miss Oakes, who had to dash off to a meeting, asked if someone would be good enough to stay behind and clean the blackboard at break-time.

Alice's hand was in the air before anyone else had a chance to raise theirs, and she remained behind in the class-room while the others went outside to get some fresh air.

'Dear me,' drawled June, a touch of malice in her tone. 'It seems that Alice is going to be a teacher's pet.'

'Don't be unkind, June!' said Felicity. 'She's probably just keen to make a good impression.'

'Yes, give her a chance,' said Susan. 'Perhaps this is Alice's way of trying to fit in.'

'Well, if she wants to make a good impression, she would be far better off running errands for us girls,' laughed Nora. 'Now, if Alice offered to do my darning that would certainly impress me!'

The others laughed at this, but they soon discovered that Alice's good deeds weren't confined to the mistresses.

At lunch, Freddie dropped her fork on the floor, and before she could bend to pick it up, Alice had retrieved it, before announcing that she would go to the kitchen and fetch her a clean one.

Then, when Delia half-jokingly said that she would love a second helping of pudding, Alice offered to give hers up.

'Oh, I couldn't possibly take your pudding, Alice,' said Delia, quite flustered. 'I eat far too many sweet things, anyway, and I'm sure that it won't hurt me to go without.'

'Oh, please take it, Delia,' said Alice, pushing her pudding plate towards the girl. 'Really, I feel full up and don't think that I can eat it.'

'Well, if you're quite sure,' Delia had said, a little reluctantly.

And Alice had insisted, a beaming smile spreading over her face as Delia began to eat. And, watching her, Felicity once again had the sensation that she had met Alice before.

Pam, sitting next to Felicity, said in a low voice, 'How very odd!'

'What is odd, Pam?' asked Felicity, turning to look at the girl.

'Well,' said Pam. 'When Alice smiled just then, I had the strangest feeling that I knew her.'

'That really *is* strange,' said Felicity. 'Because I had exactly the same feeling. And I felt it when we were on the train together, too. So did Susan, and June.'

'Really?' said Pam. 'How very peculiar! Perhaps she has a sister . . .'

'She *doesn't* have a sister who came to Malory Towers,' Felicity interrupted. 'She told us that she is an only child.'

'Oh,' said Pam, crestfallen. 'But the funniest thing of all is that when I look at Alice now, I feel quite certain that I have never seen her before.'

'Yes!' said Felicity. 'It seems to be only when she wears certain expressions that I think she seems familiar. It's very queer indeed.'

'Nonsense!' scoffed June, who had overheard all of this. 'There's nothing strange or queer about it. Alice simply reminds us of someone, and one day it will come to one of us, when we are least expecting it. We'll say, "Oh yes, she looks like that girl so-and-so, who used to be in South Tower." You'll see!'

June's explanation was so reasonable and so matter-of-fact that Pam and Felicity felt sure that she was right, and even felt a little ashamed of themselves for allowing their imaginations to run away with them.

Alice found another opportunity to help that evening.

Susan had come to Felicity's study, and the two girls were talking about the work they would have to do for Higher Cert.

'I intend to knuckle down right away,' said Susan, a determined look on her face. 'I want to get a head start.'

'Good idea,' said Felicity. 'I shall do the same, though it will seem awfully queer studying alone. I'm used to doing it in the common-room, with everyone groaning and sighing. I don't know that I shall be able to concentrate without it!'

'Well, I expect we shall soon get used to the peace and quiet,' said Susan, getting up. 'I'm off to get a couple of hours reading in now, before bed-time.'

Shortly after Susan had departed, someone tapped softly at Felicity's door, and she called out, 'Come in!'

The door was pushed open, and Alice peered round, a rather nervous smile on her face.

'Can I help you, Alice?' asked Felicity.

The girl ventured further into the room, saying rather hesitantly, 'Actually, I was hoping that *I* might be able to help *you*. You see, Felicity, I overheard you talking to Susan earlier. Not that I was eavesdropping, but your door was open and I happened to be walking past. And I thought that perhaps I could help you with your studying.'

'It's very kind of you to offer, Alice,' said Felicity, looking rather puzzled. 'But I really don't see how you *can* help.'

'Well, when I was studying for School Cert a couple of years ago, my father used to test me on how much I had learned by asking me questions,' explained Alice. 'I found that it helped me tremendously.'

'That's not a bad idea,' said Felicity, smiling. 'Sit down, Alice, and grab that history book.'

Delighted that her offer of help had been accepted, Alice sat in one of the armchairs and opened the book.

Then she began to test Felicity by asking questions, feeling very impressed indeed when the girl answered most of them correctly.

'My goodness, you're clever!' said Alice when they had finished. 'I should think that you will pass with flying colours.'

'I'm not particularly clever really,' laughed Felicity. 'Though it's very nice of you to say so. It's just that I spent a lot of time in the holidays studying. Now, June, on the other hand, is really clever – and very lucky! She has the most amazing memory, and facts just seem to stick in her head. She hardly needs to study at all.'

'Yes,' said Alice, with a laugh. 'I remember –'

Then she stopped suddenly, turning rather red, before continuing hastily, 'I remember when I was at my last school, there was a girl like June. She could read a poem once, and then recite it perfectly. How we all envied her.'

Then Alice glanced at her watch, and, jumping to her feet, said, 'Heavens, is that the time? I must go and finish my Maths prep before bedtime. I'll see you later, Felicity.'

And she dashed from the study before Felicity even had time to thank her for her help. Felicity had a feeling that Alice had been about to say something else when she had started talking about the girl at her old school, and just stopped herself in time. And, now that she came to think about it, Miss Oakes hadn't given them any Maths prep today!

How odd. And what a strange girl Alice was.

At the pool

The first week of term flew by, and soon the old girls felt as if they had never been away. Of course, it took longer for the new girls to settle in, especially the first formers.

Violet continued to irritate everyone with her boastful, conceited ways. It was quite obvious, from her expensive clothes and wonderful belongings – many of which she had brought to school with her – that the girl came from a wealthy family. And, as Daffy said, she never missed an opportunity to rub people's noses in it.

'My parents wanted to send me to a much more exclusive school,' Violet said in the dormitory one evening, looking at her surroundings with an air of disdain. 'The dormitories were so much nicer than the ones here, and even the lower school had studies of their own instead of common-rooms.'

'Well, why didn't they?' asked an outspoken girl called Ivy. 'I'm sure that you would have fitted in much better at one of those snobbish places than here, at Malory Towers.'

'Perhaps the school was a little *too* exclusive for Violet,' said Daffy slyly. 'And the Head refused to take her.'

'Nothing of the sort,' said Violet, with a haughty toss

of the head. 'If you must know, my grandmother insisted that I should be sent here. You see, she was a schoolgirl here, many, many years ago. And, when I was born, she made Daddy promise that he would send me here too. He tried to make her change her mind, so that I could go to a more superior school, but Grandmother wouldn't hear of it and held him to his word.'

'Well, at least there's one sensible person in your family,' said Katie. 'And I, for one, think that Malory Towers is a jolly fine school, although I haven't been here very long.'

The others agreed heartily, and Violet pouted crossly, turning away to pick up a silver-backed hairbrush from her bedside cabinet.

All of the first formers had personal belongings on top of their little cabinets – a photograph, a mirror, or some little trinket that they had brought from home. But Violet's cabinet was absolutely crammed with things. There was the silver-backed hairbrush and a matching mirror, a little jewellery box and various perfumes and lotions. Then there were two photographs, both in very ornate frames. One was of her beautiful Siamese cat, Willow, and the other was of Violet and her parents.

The girls had been most amused to see the family photograph, for, although Mrs Forsyth was quite a pretty woman, it was clear that Violet had inherited her looks from her father, for he had the same small eyes and snub nose.

Violet had also brought a number of dresses to school

with her and, as she hung her school uniform in her wardrobe, Daffy caught a glimpse of one hanging up. It was a pale pink party dress, festooned with frills and ribbons, and the girl couldn't think why Violet had brought it to school with her. And suddenly a wicked idea came to her.

As soon as Violet went to the bathroom, she gathered the others round and explained it to them.

'Oh, I say!' chuckled Ivy. 'What a super idea, Daffy!'

'Marvellous!' said Katie, clapping her hands together in glee. 'You are naughty, Daffy, but so funny.'

Even Faith, the quiet head-girl, giggled, though all the girls made themselves look perfectly serious when Violet returned.

'Our first Saturday at Malory Towers tomorrow night,' said Daffy, climbing into bed. 'I must say, I'm looking forward to tomorrow evening.'

'Why, what's happening tomorrow evening?' asked Violet, a puzzled look on her face.

'Don't you know?' said Katie. 'On Saturday evenings, everyone dresses up for supper. I'm going to wear the yellow dress with the satin bows that Mother made for me in the holidays. What about you, Daffy?'

'I shall wear my blue one, with the lace collar,' Daffy said. 'It really is beautiful. Violet, you simply *must* wear your pink party dress. I bet that you'll look lovely in it.'

Violet, quite unaccustomed to compliments from Daffy, looked at her a little suspiciously, but, as the others launched into descriptions of the imaginary dresses they intended to wear, her suspicions vanished and she became caught up in the excitement.

The first formers talked until long after lights out, and poor Faith simply didn't know how to stop them. At one point she ventured to say, 'No more talking, please, girls.' But her voice was so quiet that the laughter and chatter of the others quite drowned it out. In fact, they were making so much noise that no one heard footsteps approaching, or the door open. It wasn't until the light was suddenly switched on, making everyone blink, that the first formers realised Mam'zelle Dupont, who was on duty that night, had entered.

'Ah, *méchantes filles*!' she cried. 'You are very bad, to be talking after the lights have gone out. See how you disturb the poor little Daphne?'

Daffy, who had swiftly become one of Mam'zelle's favourites, was blinking and rubbing her eyes, a very disgruntled look on her face. No one would have guessed that she was the one who had been making most noise!

Mam'zelle certainly didn't, and she turned to Faith now, saying sternly, 'Faith, it is not right that you allow these bad girls to disobey the rules! As head-girl, it is your duty to see that they behave properly, and you have failed.'

'Sorry, Mam'zelle,' mumbled Faith, looking very downcast indeed.

The others began to feel a little uncomfortable. They had quickly realised that Faith was too weak to be a good leader, and had taken advantage of this. But no one wanted to get the girl into trouble.

Ivy spoke up, saying, 'We are all sorry, Mam'zelle. It wasn't Faith's fault, truly it wasn't.'

'No, she did tell us to be quiet,' said Maggie, who slept in the bed next to Faith and had heard her half-hearted attempt to remonstrate with them. 'But we took no notice.'

'Ah, you are all wicked girls, except for the dear Daphne, who has been trying to sleep,' said Mam'zelle, wagging her finger.

Faith felt that it was little unfair that Daffy, who had talked more than all the others put together, was the only one not to be scolded, but she would not dream of sneaking on the girl. Why, that was quite unthinkable!

'I do not want another sound from this dormitory tonight,' said Mam'zelle. 'I shall be back later, and if there is any noise you will all get extra French prep next week.'

No one wanted that, so as soon as the door closed behind Mam'zelle, everyone snuggled down under the bedclothes, and, as they were really very tired, it wasn't long before everyone dropped off.

Saturday dawned bright and sunny, and it was unusually warm for the time of year.

'I might go for a dip in the pool,' said June, at the breakfast table. 'Anyone care to join me?'

'I'd love to come,' said Felicity with a sigh. 'But I suppose I had better do some studying.'

Miss Oakes happened to walk by the sixth formers' table at that moment, and overhead this.

'Felicity,' she said. 'I insist that you go for a swim. In fact, I insist that *all* of you Higher Certificate girls take some time off today, for I know how hard you have been working. I positively forbid you to study!'

The girls were very pleased to hear this, for they really did feel in need of relaxation, and, as Pam said, 'We can't possibly disobey our form-mistress. I'll join you for that swim, June.'

In the end, most of the sixth formers went to the pool. Amy and Bonnie, who hated any kind of exercise, went off to Amy's study for a good gossip, while Julie and Lucy went horse-riding. Alice refused to get changed and get into the pool, saying that she wasn't a very good swimmer, but she went along with the others and sat at the side, watching them.

The girls had a very pleasant time indeed, the strong swimmers like Felicity, Susan and June doing as many lengths as they could, while others, like Delia and Nora, preferred to paddle around in the shallow end.

But their peace was rudely shattered when they were joined by a group of first formers.

'Hallo, Felicity,' said Daffy. 'Do you mind if we join you? Miss Potts said that we might swim today, as the weather is so lovely.'

The sixth formers could hardly say no, as Miss Potts had given her permission, but the pool suddenly seemed rather overcrowded with a dozen or so giggling, excited first formers splashing around.

Violet Forsyth, who looked most ungainly in her

swimming costume, stood uncertainly on the edge. She couldn't swim and was afraid of the water. The girl would much rather be indoors, but unfortunately she had made the mistake of boasting about her swimming-pool at home. Somehow the boasting had got out of hand and turned into downright lies.

The first formers had come down to see the pool on their first day and, while the others had been in raptures over it, Violet had merely shrugged, and said in a bored manner, 'I suppose it's all right, but it's nowhere near as nice as our pool at home.'

'Oh, do you have your own swimming-pool?' Katie had asked, pretending to sound most impressed. 'How marvellous!'

Encouraged by this, Violet had gone on to tell the listening girls about the marvellous garden parties her parents held in the summer, where all the guests swam in the pool.

'I'll bet you're a wonderful swimmer, Violet,' Daffy had said admiringly.

And foolish Violet, who loved nothing more than being the centre of attention, had got quite carried away, and told the first formers of how she swam several lengths in the pool every day, when the weather was warm enough.

But Daffy noticed now that the girl hung back and didn't venture too close to the edge – hardly the behaviour of someone who felt quite at home in the water. Besides, if Violet swam every day, as she claimed, surely she wouldn't be so plump, thought Daffy.

It was quite true that Violet had a swimming-pool at her home, but the girl never used it. And now she was regretting her boasting, for she had been quite unable to get out of going down to the pool with the others, and soon her lie would be exposed in front of them all.

'Come on, Violet!' Daffy called out. 'Jump in!'

Violet had no intention of jumping in, but she realised that she couldn't stand shivering on the edge forever. So she walked gingerly down the steps, fervently hoping that, amongst such a crowd, no one would notice that she wasn't actually swimming.

But Daffy's sharp eyes were watching, and she smiled to herself as she saw Violet clinging to the side in the shallow end.

Some of the sixth formers didn't care to share the pool with the boisterous youngsters and got out. Soon only Felicity, Susan and June were left, and they had to call the first formers to order on several occasions.

Violet, who had been barged into by Maggie and splashed by Ivy, had had quite enough of the pool, and decided to slip away and get dressed. No one seemed to have noticed that she wasn't joining in with the swimming, and, with luck, the weather would turn cold soon, so she wouldn't have to come down to the pool again. She had got away with it!

But Violet was quite mistaken, for Daffy spotted her getting out of the pool, and followed her.

'Not going in already, are you?' she asked. 'You haven't even been in the deep end yet.'

'I think I'm getting a cold,' said Violet, turning red. 'It's probably best if I don't swim any more today.'

Daffy grinned to herself, knowing that the girl hadn't swum at all. But she looked most concerned, and said, 'I daresay you're right. Listen, Violet, when you have changed, would you mind coming back to the pool and throwing some pennies into the water, so that I can dive for them?'

Since she had nothing better to do, and didn't really feel like sitting in the common-room on her own, Violet agreed.

The girl was soon back at the pool, fully dressed, and she stood at the side, close to Alice, calling out, 'Daffy, I have some pennies in my pocket when you are ready.'

Daffy climbed out of the pool and up on to the lowest diving board. Standing poised on the edge, she shouted, 'Throw one in now, Violet!'

Violet obliged, and Daffy did a beautiful dive into the water, causing June to say to Susan, 'That kid dives jolly well! I shall have to bear her in mind for the swimming competition next summer.'

'Yes, she's a strong swimmer, too,' said Susan, as Daffy swam to the side of the pool and stretched her arm up so that Violet could take the penny back from her.

Violet bent forward to take the coin from Daffy, feeling rather nervous, for she didn't like being so close to the edge.

And suddenly, the girl felt Daffy's hand close round her wrist in a firm grip, there was a tug on her arm, and Violet felt herself being pulled towards the deep water. Instinctively, she flailed about with her free hand, trying to find something to hold on to. Alas, the only thing was poor Alice! Somehow, Violet managed to seize her ankle as she was falling into the water, and the whole thing was like some terrible chain reaction, as, with a squeal of terror, Violet fell into the pool, and Alice fell in right behind her.

Violet sank like a stone, and although Alice could swim a little, she didn't like the deep end, and the weight of her clothes was dragging her down.

June and Susan, taking in all that had happened in a glance, went to the aid of the two girls at once. Felicity, at the other end of the pool, didn't realise what was happening at first, but as soon as she heard the commotion she swam down to the deep end and helped Susan get the shocked Alice to the surface and out of the pool.

'Are you all right, Alice?' asked Felicity, as the girl sat down on the ground, gasping for air.

Quite unable to speak, Alice could only nod, and Susan said, 'Let her get her breath back, then we had better get her to Matron. Violet, too.'

'Here are your glasses, Alice,' said Felicity, who had found them at the edge of the pool. 'They must have slipped off when you fell in.'

Alice took them from her, and, in the split second before she put them on, Felicity felt that little stirring of recognition again. Then, once Alice's glasses were on her nose again, it vanished. Felicity gave herself a little shake, telling herself sternly that she was making far too much out of it, and it was as June had said – Alice merely reminded her of someone. There were far more important things to think about now, anyway.

It had taken all of June's strength to pull Violet to the surface, for the girl was plump and heavy. Felicity helped June to get her out of the pool, and they laid her on the ground.

Violet was still, her eyes closed, and, for a moment, Daffy thought that her heart would stop in fright. It had only been a prank, she had just meant to scare Violet, not do her any harm.

Then, to Daffy's tremendous relief, the girl opened her eyes and began to sob noisily.

'Well, there can't be much wrong with her if she can cry so loudly,' said June drily. Then she turned to Daffy and said sternly, 'That was a very dangerous prank, which could have had serious consequences if we sixth formers hadn't been around.'

Daffy's knees trembled, for she was a little in awe of the games captain.

'Whatever do you mean, June?' asked Felicity, quite astonished. 'Surely you aren't suggesting that Daffy pushed Violet and Alice in.'

'She didn't push Violet, she pulled her,' said June grimly. 'I saw her. Poor Alice just happened to get in the way.'

'It's true, Felicity,' said Susan, seeing her friend's look of disbelief. 'I saw Daffy deliberately pull Violet into the water as well.'

Felicity was quite speechless, so June said, 'Whatever were you thinking about, Daffy, to pull a girl who can't swim into the deep end? You must have known how dangerous it was.'

'We didn't know that Violet couldn't swim,' piped up Katie, in defence of her friend. 'She is always bragging to us about her swimming-pool at home, and telling us what a marvellous swimmer she is.'

Daffy said nothing, for she had realised that Violet couldn't swim, yet she had plunged her into the deep end anyway. June was quite right – she *hadn't* stopped to think how grave the consequences could have been.

Fortunately for Daffy, however, June had now turned her attention to the still-sobbing Violet, who was sitting up now. June said firmly, 'Do stop crying! Violet, is this true? Did you lead the girls to believe that you could swim?'

With the eyes of the first form upon her, Violet turned red and kept her eyes down, as she muttered, 'Yes.'

'Well, what a foolish thing to do!' said Felicity scornfully. 'I hope that you see now, Violet, what trouble lies can lead to.'

'How was I to know that that mean beast Daffy would pull me in?' cried Violet, feeling that it was rather too bad that she was getting a share of the blame as well.

'Daffy will be punished, you may be sure of that,' said Felicity. Then she glanced at June, saying, 'But I think that a few extra swimming lessons for Violet may be in order?'

'Exactly what I was thinking,' said June with a grim

smile. 'Violet, please come to my study this afternoon and we will make out a time-table.'

Poor Violet groaned inwardly, but she did not dare disobey June. She would find a way of paying Daffy Hope back for this.

'And you, Daffy, will come to *my* study this afternoon,' said Felicity, sounding unusually annoyed, for she felt very disappointed in Daffy. 'Where I shall give you a suitable punishment.'

'Yes, Felicity,' said Daffy, looking and sounding very subdued indeed.

But, now that she knew that Violet was going to be all right, Daffy felt quite unworried. She felt certain that Felicity, who had known her family for years, would not come down on her too hard.

In fact, Violet had come off very much worse, for, as well as her unexpected dip in the pool, she now had to face the prospect of extra swimming lessons with June!

As Felicity, Susan and June bore the two dripping wet girls off to Matron's room, Daffy smiled to herself.

Everything was going her way! She was ruling the roost in the first form, and had convinced most of the mistresses that she was a good, sweet girl. Pulling the wool over Felicity's eyes would be too easy for words!

Daffy in trouble

'Good heavens!' exclaimed Matron, getting up from her chair as the little group entered her room. 'Whatever has happened?'

'An accident at the swimming-pool, Matron,' said Felicity. 'Alice and Violet fell in.'

Violet seethed, for it had been no accident and she opened her mouth to say so. Then June gave her a nudge, and a stern look of warning. Violet knew at once what June was trying to tell her – that it wasn't done to sneak.

And Violet didn't really want to be sent to Coventry by the rest of her form, for it was pleasant to have people to boast to, even though the others never seemed very impressed. So she said nothing, and decided that she would find some other way of getting even with Daffy Hope.

Matron was bustling about now, putting the kettle on and giving the two girls blankets.

'Go into the little bathroom there and get out of those wet things at once,' she said briskly. 'Then wrap those blankets around yourselves while I make some nice, hot tea. When you have both warmed up a little I shall check that you have suffered no ill effects.'

Clutching their blankets, Alice and Violet trooped off

to the bathroom, and Matron turned to the others.

'An accident, you say?' she said, sounding most suspicious. 'Well, I expect the first formers to fool around by the swimming-pool, but I am most surprised to find a sixth former involved.'

'Alice really did get knocked in by accident, Matron,' said Susan. 'She wasn't fooling around.'

'Well, I'm pleased to hear it,' said Matron. 'Now, don't stand there dripping all over my floor! Off you go, and get changed.'

The three girls were still in their swimming costumes, for they had wanted to get Alice and Violet to Matron's room as quickly as possible.

Now they were beginning to feel a little chilly themselves, so they sped off back to the changing-rooms.

'I could do with a nice, hot cup of tea myself,' said Felicity as they dressed. 'Let's all go back to my study and I'll put the kettle on.'

This was a very welcome suggestion indeed, and the three girls made their way to Felicity's study. They passed Bonnie's study on the way, and, as her door was open, they could see the girl hard at work inside, her curly head bent over a book as she scribbled down notes.

'My word, Bonnie really is taking this seriously,' said Susan. 'I say, Bonnie! Didn't you hear what Miss Oakes said? We are supposed to take today off.'

'You can overdo it, you know,' said June. 'I thought that you and Amy were going to spend some time together?'

'Well, we had a lovely chat while you were down at the pool,' said Bonnie. 'Then I thought that I could get a head start on you others by studying today while you are all enjoying yourselves.'

'Well, not only has Miss Oakes forbidden it, but I forbid it, too,' said Felicity with mock-sternness. 'We really do need to relax every now and then, you know, Bonnie, then we can go back to our studying feeling refreshed.'

'Yes, come along to Felicity's study with us, and have a cup of tea,' said June, taking Bonnie's arm and pulling her up from her chair.

Amy, who was feeling very bored and lost without her little friend, came along then, and Felicity cried, 'Amy! We are trying to persuade Bonnie not to work so hard, and would be very grateful if you would add your word to ours.'

'I already have,' said Amy, sounding rather disgruntled. 'Really, Bonnie, I don't see that taking one day off from your studies would do any harm. We could go into town after lunch and spend our pocket money. Then we could have tea in the little tea-shop. My treat.'

Bonnie's eyes lit up at this, and she said, 'That would be fun, I must say.'

'Well, that's settled, then,' said June cheerfully, leading Bonnie from the room. 'We are all having a day off, even you, Bonnie.'

'Yes, come on, let's get that kettle on, Felicity,' said Susan. 'I'm simply dying for a cup of tea.'

In the end there was quite a crowd in Felicity's study, for Amy came along too, and they were also joined by Alice, who had been given a clean bill of health by Matron. Felicity had to perch on the window-sill, but she didn't mind at all, for it was nice to be with her friends, and to laugh and joke with them.

Alice was the first to leave, saying that she had to write a letter to her parents, and, as the door closed behind her, Susan said, 'Alice never says much about her parents, or her home life, does she?'

'Well, she's rather shy,' said Felicity. 'Perhaps we should ask her, and try to draw her out a little.'

'It's obvious that her parents are very wealthy,' said Amy unexpectedly.

'Is it?' said June, surprised. 'Not to me it isn't. I mean to say, she doesn't have any marvellous possessions, or boast about how rich her family are. Unlike some people.'

Amy, who knew that this was aimed at her, flushed. Her parents were very wealthy indeed, and she liked to make sure that people knew it.

'Her clothes are very expensive,' said Amy, rather stiffly. 'I can tell, for some of them come from the same shops I get mine from. And she has a handbag in her wardrobe exactly like one I have at home. Mother bought it for my birthday last year, and it cost an awful lot of money.'

Amy knew about such things, so the others believed her words, and it made them even more curious about the new girl.

At last the others drifted away and only Felicity and Susan remained in the study.

'What punishment are you going to give young Daffy Hope?' asked Susan curiously. 'I suppose that it's difficult for you, what with your family and hers being such close friends.'

'I have made up my mind that I will treat Daffy exactly as I would any of the other kids,' said Felicity firmly. 'It certainly wouldn't be just or fair to show her any favouritism. She must apologise to both Violet and Alice, of course, and I shall forbid her to leave the school grounds next Saturday.'

'If you ask me, she's getting off quite lightly,' said Susan.

'Ah, but you see, the first formers are planning a picnic on the beach next Saturday, if the weather is fine,' said Felicity, with a smile. 'Imagine how young Daffy will feel, watching the others go off to enjoy themselves, while she has to remain at school alone.'

'All right, I take that back,' said Susan. 'Daffy isn't getting off lightly at all! Let's just hope it makes her think twice before playing such a dangerous trick again.'

Daffy knocked on the door of Felicity's study at three o'clock, and, on being told to come in, was surprised to see Alice and Violet there. And she didn't like the malicious, slightly triumphant look that Violet gave her at all!

Felicity had asked the two girls along, for she wanted to be sure that Daffy apologised to them both. Alice had been a little reluctant, saying, 'Oh, but Daffy didn't cause me to fall into the water deliberately, Felicity. I should feel most uncomfortable if you made her apologise to me.'

But Felicity had stood firm. 'The kid needs to learn to think about the consequences of her actions. You falling in was one of those consequences, and I insist that she says sorry to you,' she had said.

Violet, of course, had needed no persuading, quite delighted to think that her arch-enemy would have to apologise to her under the stern eye of the Head Girl.

'Daffy,' said Felicity coolly. 'I trust that you have now had time to think about your behaviour?'

Daffy, at her most demure, nodded and said meekly, 'Yes, Felicity. It was very bad of me, and I shall never, ever do such a thing again.'

'I am pleased to hear it,' said Felicity. 'Now, before I give you your punishment, I think that you have something to say to Alice and Violet.'

Daffy, realising at once what Felicity wanted her to do, wasn't at all pleased! She didn't mind saying sorry to Alice – indeed, she had intended to do so before Felicity had prompted her. But apologising to that hateful Violet, who was certain to gloat, was quite another matter.

But, glancing at Felicity's determined expression, Daffy realised that she really didn't have any choice in the matter.

'Alice, I'm most awfully sorry,' she said sincerely, looking up at the bigger girl. 'I really didn't mean for you to fall into the pool as well. I had no idea that Violet would grab hold of you like that.'

Alice accepted the apology graciously, then Daffy turned to Violet.

'*Dear* Violet,' she said, making her tone sickly-sweet. 'I simply don't know what came over me, and I hope that you, too, will accept my most sincere apologies. But some good has come out of it, for June is going to teach you to swim, and I know how much you will enjoy that.'

Of course, Daffy knew quite well that the girl was dreading the swimming lessons, and Violet, realising this, scowled at her. Felicity, however, noticed nothing amiss, and felt pleased that Daffy had apologised so sincerely and so readily.

'Violet?' she said.

Violet would have liked nothing better than to refuse Daffy's apology, but she knew that it would earn her a scold from Felicity, so she accepted it rather stiffly, a sullen expression on her face.

'Well,' said Alice, looking rather relieved as she edged towards the door, 'I shall go back to my study now.'

'You can go too, Violet,' said Felicity.

Violet, who had hoped that she would be able to stay and hear what Daffy's punishment was to be, looked rather put out, but followed Alice from the room.

As the door closed behind the two girls, Felicity turned to Daffy, staring hard at the girl. Looking at the first former's sweet face and innocent expression, it was hard to believe that she was capable of any mischief whatsoever. As far as Felicity was concerned, Daffy's behaviour at the pool that morning was completely out of character, and hopefully the punishment she was about to dish out would ensure that it was not repeated.

Felicity got out the little punishment book that all the top formers carried with them, and wrote something on one of the slips in her neat handwriting. Then she tore it out and handed it to the first former.

Daffy took it, thinking what a bore it was that she would have to give up some of her free time to write out lines, or learn a poem or something. Then her face fell as she looked at the punishment slip.

'But we first formers are going for a picnic next Saturday!' wailed Daffy, looking at Felicity in dismay. 'If I'm confined to school, that means I shall miss it.'

Felicity couldn't help feeling a little sorry for the girl, but she was determined to stick to her word, and said crisply, 'Well, perhaps you should have thought about that before pulling Violet into the swimming-pool! I am sorry, Daffy, but the punishment stands. You may go now.'

Scowling every bit as darkly as Violet had a few minutes earlier, Daffy left the study. She would have liked to slam the door behind her, but didn't dare. Felicity might call her back and give her another punishment!

Halfway down the corridor, she stopped and looked at the punishment slip again, her mind racing. It wasn't just the severity of the punishment that bothered her, but the fact that she had boasted to the others about how Felicity was a friend of the family, and would be sure to let her off lightly. Now she would lose face in front of the first form, and that silly Violet would crow over her like anything! Then a thought came to Daffy. There was no need to tell the others about her punishment, for if she went on the picnic Felicity would never know!

So when she joined the others in the first-form common-room, and they crowded round to ask what her punishment had been, Daffy laughed and said cheerfully, 'Felicity let me off scot-free. Didn't I tell you that she wouldn't come down hard on me?'

'That's hardly fair,' protested Ivy, frowning. 'I'm sure if it had been one of us others we would have been punished.'

'Well, I did have a small punishment,' admitted Daffy. 'I had to apologise to Her Highness. And to Alice, of course, but I didn't mind that.'

'It must have been dreadful saying sorry to Her Highness, though,' said Katie, sympathetically. 'No wonder she has been looking so smug!'

Violet, who was sitting in an armchair reading a book, overheard this and glared at Katie, who promptly stuck out her tongue at the girl.

Daffy pulled Katie aside, saying in a low voice, 'Listen, Katie, I'm going to tell you something, but you mustn't let any of the others know. Promise?'

'Of course,' said Katie at once. 'You can count on me.'

Quickly Daffy told Katie that Felicity had forbidden her to go on the picnic, and Katie gasped, 'Oh, no! I didn't think that Felicity would be so harsh.'

'Nor did I,' said Daffy with a grimace. 'But it doesn't

matter, for I'm going anyway. Felicity will never find out.'

'I certainly hope not, for your sake,' said Katie, torn between shock that Daffy was going to disobey the Head Girl and ignore her punishment, and admiration at her daring. 'If she does, you'll be for the high jump all right!'

'Pooh!' said Daffy, tossing her dark curls. 'Who cares for Felicity and the rest of those stuffy sixth formers? I came to Malory Towers to have some fun, and that's exactly what I intend to do!'

Trouble in the first form

There was more trouble for Violet at supper that evening. The first formers watched, trying hard to hide their smiles, as Violet got out her beautiful pink dress and laid it carefully on the bed.

The girl saw the others staring, and said, 'Aren't you going to get changed?'

'There's plenty of time,' said Daffy. 'I'm going to have a bath first.'

'And I need to wash my hands,' said Katie. 'I don't want to get dirty marks on my lovely party dress.'

'I wonder if I have time to wash my hair?' said Maggie.

The others had planned this carefully, for they wanted to make sure that Violet was the last to use the bathroom.

'She always spends ages titivating herself,' Daffy had said. 'If we can time it so that she is in the bathroom when the bell goes for tea, the rest of us can be gone by the time she comes out, and she won't realise that she is the only one who is dressed up like a dog's dinner!'

Violet was rather disgruntled to be the last one in the bathroom, but there was little she could do about it.

'Don't take too long, Violet,' called Ivy, as the girl, at

last, made her way to the bathroom. 'The rest of us are about to get into all our finery.'

But, of course, the first formers didn't get into their finery at all! As it was a Saturday, they were allowed to wear their own clothes, but no one dressed for supper at all. All of the girls wore quite plain dresses, or jumpers with skirts or trousers.

'Her Highness is going to stick out like a sore thumb,' chuckled Katie, rubbing her hands together in glee.

'Let's make our way to the dining-room now,' said Daffy. 'We want to make absolutely certain that we are out of the way when Violet comes back in, or the whole trick will be ruined.'

So, when Violet entered the dormitory, just after the bell had sounded for supper, she was very surprised indeed to find it empty.

'Mean beasts!' she thought, slipping the flounced, frilly dress over her head. 'They might have waited for me.'

But, as she admired herself in the mirror, Violet came to realise that, perhaps, it was a good thing the others had gone in to tea without her. She would be able to make a grand entrance, and every eye would be upon her.

And Violet was quite right, for every eye *was* upon her – but not for the reason she had hoped!

Miss Potts, sitting at the mistresses' table, was the first to spot the girl, and her jaw dropped.

The mistress had very little time for what she termed fripperies, and she frowned heavily. Really, what a silly girl Violet was, dressing up as if she were attending some grand party! Did she really think that by doing so she would make people admire her? Instead, she had made herself look quite ridiculous.

Then the sixth formers spotted her, and Freddie, taking a sip of tea, choked.

'My word!' gasped Gillian. 'What a sight!'

A peal of laughter came from the first-form table, and June cast a sidelong glance at Daffy Hope. The girl's eyes were brimming with mischief, a broad grin on her face as she gazed at Violet, before whispering something to Katie.

At once, June realised what had happened. Those wicked first formers had tricked Violet into making herself look silly. And if Daffy wasn't at the back of it, she would be very surprised indeed!

Of course, the sixth formers no longer played such childish tricks, but, as June saw the dawning horror on Violet's face, she couldn't help wishing that she had thought of this one when she was younger, for it was really very funny.

Unsurprisingly, poor Violet didn't think it was at all funny! She had walked into the dining-room with her head held high, looking very pleased with herself indeed. But it hadn't take her long to realise that she was the only girl wearing a party dress, or to see the grins of amusement on the faces around her. The girl turned as red as a beetroot, wishing that the floor would open up and swallow her.

The shrewd Miss Potts, seeing the girl's look of dismay and confusion, and the mirth of the first formers, also realised that Violet had somehow been tricked. She got to her feet.

'Come along, Violet,' she said, taking the girl's arm and leading her across to the first-form table. 'It is nice to see that *one* of my form has taken the trouble to make herself look nice. Ivy, you don't appear to have brushed your hair at all! And Daphne, I see that you have already managed to spill tea over your skirt.'

This was said loudly enough for several people nearby to overhear, and June grinned to herself as Daffy turned red. Ah, the first former might be able to fool silly little Violet, but she would never get one over on Miss Potts!

Daffy had, indeed, turned red and, as Violet slipped into an empty seat beside Faith, and Miss Potts went back to her own table, she muttered to Katie, 'Potty didn't really mean that about Violet looking nice, you know, for she has no time for people who fuss over their appearance. She only said it to try and make the rest of us feel small.'

'You must admit that she's jolly sharp, though,' said Katie, looking at the mistress in awe. 'She obviously realises that we were behind the whole thing.'

Violet, of course, was delighted that Daffy had found herself on the receiving end of Miss Potts's sharp tongue. Her feelings were soothed still further when Faith, who felt a little guilty about the trick, said softly, 'You really do look nice, Violet. Personally, I think it's a pity that we *don't* all get dressed up on a Saturday evening.'

Mam'zelle Dupont, at the head of the first-form table, also thoroughly approved of Violet's appearance.

'The good Miss Potts is quite right,' she declared. 'It is nice to see young people looking their best. Now, when I return to *la belle* France, and have dinner with my so-dear family, my nieces and nephews always wear their finest clothes. That is how it should be.'

And at once Mam'zelle launched into a string of anecdotes about her beloved nieces and nephews, which bored most of the first formers heartily, but which they were forced to listen to politely.

Violet, however, began to feel that the whole episode hadn't been such a disaster after all. She was in the good books of both Mam'zelle and Miss Potts, and that horrid Daffy had been scolded as well. So Violet ate her supper quite happily, listening with the appearance of interest to Mam'zelle's tales, and enjoying the disgruntled expressions on the faces of the others.

'Well, that didn't go quite as well as I had hoped,' said Daffy glumly as the first formers left the hall. 'And, worst of all, I feel as if Violet has somehow come out on top.'

'Cheer up!' said Katie, clapping her on the back. 'It was jolly funny at first, when it suddenly dawned on Violet that she was the only one who looked as if she was going to a party. If only Miss Potts hadn't interfered, all would have been well.'

But worse was to come. On Monday morning, Miss Potts sent Violet to take a message to Miss Parker, of the second form, and as the door closed behind the girl, she got to her feet, looking at her class very sternly indeed.

'Please listen, everyone,' said the mistress, her tone so

crisp and authoritative that there wasn't a girl in the room who didn't pay attention. Even Daffy sat up straight in her chair, her gaze fixed on the mistress.

'That was a marvellous trick you played on Violet the other day,' she began. 'Even though it was rather a mean one, in my opinion. It has also come to my attention that there was an incident at the swimming-pool on the same morning, which involved Violet and one of the sixth formers falling into the pool and having to be rescued.'

Miss Potts's eyes rested on Daffy for a moment, and the girl tried to stop herself from turning red.

'However,' Miss Potts continued, 'I understand that the culprit has already been punished by Felicity Rivers, so I will say no more about the dangers of such horseplay. What I *will* say, however, is that I will not stand for any more nonsense. I understand that not all of you like Violet, but as you go through life you will meet all sorts of people, and will find that it is not possible to like each and every one of them. But, for the sake of harmony, it is necessary that you learn to get along with them. I trust that there will be no more tricks played on Violet, for if I hear about it I will dish out a very severe punishment. Is that quite clear?'

'Yes, Miss Potts,' chorused the girls in very subdued tones.

Violet came back then, so Miss Potts let the matter drop, but the girls discussed it at break-time.

'You will have to stop playing tricks on Violet now, Daffy,' said Faith, with what authority she could muster.

But Daffy merely said scornfully, 'No such thing. I shall just have to be more careful, that's all. Her Highness is such a marvellous victim!'

'Absolutely!' said Katie, backing her friend up, as always. 'Besides, Violet deserves another trick because of the way she spoke to Daffy on Saturday night.'

When the first formers had gathered in the common-room after supper on the fateful night, the others had quite expected Violet to go and change out of her party dress, but she had sat in one of the big armchairs, a vision in pink frills, and picked up a book.

'Aren't you going to change, Violet?' Ivy had asked.

'Why should I?' Violet had said, a stubborn look coming over her round face. 'I am perfectly satisfied with the way I look. So were Miss Potts and Mam'zelle. Why, even Faith said that I looked very nice.'

At once, everyone turned accusing eyes on Faith, who turned red. Though, she thought, there was no reason at all for her to feel guilty. She had only been trying to make Violet feel a little less uncomfortable.

'I must say, the colour does suit you,' Daffy had drawled. 'When you're angry your cheeks go all pink, and the dress matches them perfectly!'

Then Violet had flung down her book and got to her feet, saying angrily, 'Well, you look like a – a mop, with those silly, untidy curls all over the place! You think you're so wonderful, don't you, Daffy Hope? Just because your sister used to come here, and you know the Head Girl! Well, just you remember that pride comes before a

65

fall, and I promise you, I shall get back at you for trying to trick me tonight!'

'*Trying* to trick you?' laughed Daffy, quite unmoved by the girl's anger. 'I would say that I succeeded very nicely. Wouldn't you, girls?'

Of course, the others agreed with Daffy at once, apart from Faith, who said nothing at all.

The row had ended with Violet flouncing off to bed, but the only person she upset by doing that was herself, for she was far too angry to sleep, and soon became very bored indeed!

Faith thought of this now, as she watched the others crowding round Daffy, all of them most impressed by her boldness and daring.

Faith herself, however, was beginning to find Daffy a little tiresome. She didn't resent the girl's popularity, for lively, amusing people like Daffy always *were* popular. But she disliked the way that the girl dismissed everything that she said, and didn't seem to recognise that she was head of the form. And the others, eager to copy Daffy in everything, were following suit.

Well, it was her own fault, she supposed, for being a weak character. The first form needed a strong leader, and, as it didn't have one, it was inevitable that someone would step into the breach. Not for the first time, Faith wondered if the honourable thing to do would be to go to Miss Potts and resign, for there was no denying that she wasn't making a very good job of things.

But just then, Daffy glanced round and spotted Faith

standing on the edge of things as always, a rather forlorn expression on her face. And since, despite her mischievous ways, she was a kind-hearted girl, she moved across to her, taking her arm in a friendly way, and saying, 'Come on, Faith, old girl! There's just time for a quick ball game before Geography. You'll play, won't you?'

Katie and one or two others added their voices to Daffy's, and suddenly Faith felt a warm glow spread over her, her gloomy feelings dropping away. The first formers weren't a bad lot, at heart. She would just have to find her own way of dealing with them, and of carrying out her responsibilities as head-girl.

'Yes, you come along with us, Faith,' cried Katie, taking her other arm. 'Let's go and have some fun!'

Alice's puzzling behaviour

The first formers might be having fun, but those sixth formers who were studying for Higher Certificate were working very hard indeed.

Alice, as always, was eager to help, but not everyone appreciated her well-meaning efforts.

Pam was most grateful when the girl offered to post a letter for her, so that she could carry on with her studying. June, however, was extremely displeased to enter her study one afternoon, only to discover that someone had tidied it.

'I say!' she cried. 'What on earth has happened here? Someone has tidied all my papers away.'

'Well, you must admit that it did *need* tidying,' said Freddie, coming in behind her and looking at the neatly arranged desk. 'Why, there was so much stuff on there before, you couldn't even *see* the desk.'

'Yes, but although it might have looked a mess to everyone else, *I* knew exactly where everything was!' said June, sounding very dismayed. 'My lists of teams for sports were in that corner, my English work was there, and my Maths there. I like working in a jumble. Now how am I supposed to find anything?'

It didn't take long for June to discover that Alice was the culprit, and she wasted no time in setting the girl straight.

'Look here, Alice,' she said. 'I don't appreciate you coming into my study without my permission and messing about with my things.'

'I – I'm sorry, June,' said Alice meekly. 'I was only trying to help.'

'Well, I have had to waste precious time in finding everything that you tidied away and putting it back where it was,' said June shortly. 'So you haven't helped me at all. Run round after the others if you want to, but leave me alone!'

Felicity, who overheard this, took June to task, saying, 'You were a little hard on Alice, June. She meant well.'

'I daresay,' said June. 'But I can't bear people trying to organise me! To be honest, Felicity, she gives me the creeps, always hovering around.'

Felicity protested at this, but she knew what June meant. There was an unwritten rule that if a study door was open, it meant that the occupant was 'at home' – as Susan put it – to visitors. If the door was closed, it meant that whoever was in there didn't want to be disturbed. Most of the girls kept their doors open, for it made them feel more united, and created a friendly atmosphere. But Alice had a disconcerting habit of suddenly appearing in people's doorways.

On one occasion she had quite startled Felicity, who had been completely engrossed in her work. Then she had looked up and seen Alice standing there, and almost jumped out of her skin.

'Alice!' she had gasped. 'Goodness, you gave me quite a fright!'

'I'm so sorry, Felicity,' Alice had said. 'I just came to see if there was any way that I could help you.'

Felicity, who was getting on very well on her own, didn't quite know what to say. She didn't want to spurn Alice, for the girl was so very eager to please. On the other hand, she badly wanted to pass Higher Certificate, and she couldn't allow Alice to interfere with that.

In the end she compromised by asking Alice to copy out some notes that she had scribbled down in class, for they really were difficult to read and Alice's handwriting was very neat.

But the incident quite destroyed her concentration, and when the good-natured Pam complained that she was tired of Alice constantly interrupting her studies, Felicity decided that something must be done.

'I don't quite like to push her off altogether,' said Pam. 'For I was very grateful when she cleaned my shoes the other day. It seems mean to make use of her when it suits us, then tell her to go away when we don't want her.'

'Yes, it's tricky,' said Felicity. 'I suppose the poor girl feels at a bit of a loose end, for we are all so busy studying that none of us has really got the time to get to know her.'

'We're not *all* studying,' Pam pointed out. 'Nora isn't going in for Higher Cert, and nor are Amy and Delia.'

'Why didn't I think of that?' exclaimed Felicity. 'We can ask those three to take Alice under their wing a bit.'

Pam laughed, and said, 'Nora and Delia might agree, but I can't see you having much joy with Amy. Apart from Bonnie, she looks down on everyone, and I can't see why she would treat Alice any differently.'

'I'm not so sure,' said Felicity thoughtfully. 'Amy seems to think that Alice's family are wealthy, so she may consider her worthy of her friendship.'

And it seemed that Felicity was right. She and Pam spoke to Nora, Delia and Amy later that day about Alice, and all three of them agreed that they would do what they could to befriend the new girl. But, to the astonishment of the sixth formers, it seemed to be Amy who was making the most effort, for Alice was constantly in and out of the girl's study over the next few days.

'Well, it seems that you were right, Felicity,' said Pam. 'I'm not sure that I approve of Amy's reasons for becoming Alice's friend, if she is only doing it because of her supposed wealth. But at least Alice seems happy.'

'I don't care what Amy's reason is,' said June, overhearing this. 'As long as she is keeping Alice occupied and out of our way!'

But none of the girls guessed what was behind Amy's kindness to the new girl, until Felicity peeped into the girl's study one evening, and was astonished to see her doing a pile of mending.

'Heavens, Alice!' she cried. 'There's enough mending

there to keep you busy for a week! Whatever have you been doing?'

'Oh, it's not all mine,' said Alice. 'Some of it is Amy's. She so dislikes doing it, and I am only too pleased to be able to help.'

Felicity frowned at this, for it was the rule at Malory Towers that the girls did their own mending.

She said as much, and Alice flushed, saying, 'Well, I couldn't bear to see poor Amy struggling with her mending, knowing that I could do it more quickly and so much better.'

Felicity, who knew that Amy was very good indeed at getting out of the little jobs she didn't want to do, frowned, and, noticing this, Alice said, 'Oh, please don't say that I mustn't do it, Felicity! Amy was so grateful to me, and I should feel that I was letting her down.'

'Well, as you're so keen, I shan't try to stop you,' said Felicity. 'But don't let Amy make a slave of you, Alice.'

'I shan't,' promised Alice.

Over the next few days, though, it became clear that Amy *was* taking advantage of Alice.

It was Amy's turn to do the flowers in the classroom that week, and Gillian, who came in to get a book from her desk, was most surprised to see Alice doing them instead.

'Amy is busy with something,' Alice had explained, when Gillian questioned her. But, a few minutes later, Gillian had seen Amy, strolling arm in arm through the grounds with Bonnie, not looking at all busy!

Julie, going into the dormitory after prep one evening, was taken aback to find Alice going through Amy's bedside cabinet.

'It's quite all right,' said Alice, turning red as she saw the suspicious look on Julie's face. 'Amy sent me to fetch her face cream.'

'Well, I don't see why Amy can't fetch it herself,' said Julie in her blunt way. 'Spoilt, lazy creature.'

Then Bonnie popped into Amy's study one evening, and was surprised to find Alice tidying up in there.

'Thank you so much, Alice,' said Amy with a dazzling smile when the girl had finished.

'Dear Alice,' she murmured to Bonnie, as the girl left the room. 'How she loves making herself useful.'

'And how you love making use of her,' said Bonnie drily.

'I think it's rather decent of me,' said Amy with a righteous air. 'I'm stopping her from getting on everyone else's nerves, and making her feel needed.'

'I suppose that's true,' said Bonnie, amused at her friend's reasoning. 'Make the most of her while you have her, though, for I know that Felicity doesn't approve of you taking advantage of Alice. Once Higher Cert is over, she is sure to step in and put a stop to it.'

Felicity didn't approve of Amy's behaviour at all, but with her responsibilities as Head Girl, and all her extra studying, she scarcely had time to think about the problem, let alone solve it.

June was also very busy for, as games captain, she had

to coach the younger girls, pick lacrosse teams and arrange matches with other schools. There had also been her swimming lessons with Violet. Fortunately, June didn't need to spend as much time studying as the others, for she was blessed with an amazing memory and got very good results with the minimum of effort.

Daffy Hope, who was small and very agile, had a natural talent for lacrosse, and June would have liked to choose her for one of the teams. But the girl played the fool too much, and June decided that, until she settled down a bit, she could not pick her.

'Gather round, everyone!' called June, at the end of a practice session with the first and second formers. 'And I will tell you who I have chosen to be in the lower-school team for the match against Marlowe Hall.'

The girls gathered round eagerly, their faces shining in anticipation, and June began to read out a list of names. The lucky girls whose names were called turned red with delight, as they were cheered and thumped on the back by their friends. Ivy and Katie, of the first form, were simply thrilled when June told them that they were in the team, and Katie murmured to Daffy, 'You're certain to be in, old girl, for you are a much better player than Ivy or me.'

But Daffy's name wasn't mentioned at all, even when June told the girls who the reserves were.

And, rather to her own surprise, the girl felt very hurt, and rather humiliated, for she knew that she was far better at lacrosse than at least half of the girls who had been chosen. She simply couldn't understand why June had overlooked her, and wondered if she should ask the games captain. But then, June might think that she was awfully conceited. Besides, she didn't want the games captain to know how much she cared!

Daffy hung back as the others went to get changed, all of them chattering excitedly, and June called her over.

'Daffy, you are wondering why you weren't chosen for the team, aren't you?' said June, getting straight to the point. She was extremely shrewd, and had seen the hurt and confusion on the girl's face when her name hadn't been called out. 'Well, I will tell you. It is because you fool around too much. Now, I was much the same at your age, so I am not criticising you for it. But the thing is, it's my responsibility to choose the best team to represent Malory Towers, and that means I can't have anyone on there who is going to act the goat at a crucial moment.'

Daffy felt very downcast at this, but she wasn't about to let June know, so she shrugged, and said with her usual cheery smile, 'Oh well, never mind. I daresay it would have been an awful bore having to attend all those extra practices anyway.'

June stared after Daffy as the girl walked away, whistling a cheerful little tune. Daffy *did* mind, she thought. She minded a lot. June knew this, because the first former reminded her very much of herself when she had been in the lower school.

Daffy had a lot of hard lessons to learn before she became a responsible, trustworthy person, and Malory

Towers was certainly the right place to learn them! June sincerely hoped that it wouldn't be too long before the girl found a sense of pride in her school, and a little team spirit.

But it wasn't in Daffy's nature to be downhearted for long. On the whole, she was having a marvellous time at Malory Towers, and there was still so much to look forward to. There was Mam'zelle to play tricks on, Violet to annoy, birthdays coming up – and, of course, the picnic on the beach tomorrow. Daffy was anticipating this eagerly, for the fact that she was disobeying Felicity made it all the more thrilling, and gave an edge to her excitement.

Violet, who had a great deal of pocket money, had ordered a simply enormous chocolate cake for the picnic, which she was going to collect from the baker's shop the following morning. She couldn't resist boasting to the others about it as they came out of the changing-rooms.

'It's simply magnificent,' she said. 'And cost an absolute fortune. But Daddy said that I am to spend as much as I like, and if I run short of money he will send me more.'

The others rolled their eyes, and Ivy said, 'But how will you ever learn to manage your money responsibly if you always go to your father every time it runs out?'

Violet gave a little laugh, and said, 'My family is so wealthy that I don't need to worry about things like that. All I need to think about is how to spend it.'

Alice happened to be walking by at this moment, and she stopped dead on hearing Violet's words.

'Violet!' she said in an unusually sharp tone. 'May I have a word with you, please?'

Violet looked rather surprised, but went over to Alice at once, while the rest of the first formers walked off.

Alice looked at the girl, noticing her small, spiteful-looking eyes, her smug expression, and general air of being very pleased with herself indeed. Here was someone who badly needed taking down a peg or two!

'Violet,' she began. 'I couldn't help overhearing what you were saying to the others just now. And let me tell you, you won't win any friends by boasting about your wealth.'

Violet turned red, and said rather stiffly, 'I can't help it if my father has lots of money.'

'No, but you can stop yourself ramming it down the others' throats,' said Alice. 'I can't make you stop boasting, of course, I can only advise you. If you want to be happy at Malory Towers, give the girls your warmth and your friendship, don't try and win them over with your wealth.'

Violet had nothing to say to this and, as she walked away, Alice sighed to herself. She doubted very much that the girl would change overnight, but hoped that she would listen to her words, and act on them. Suddenly a voice right behind her called her name, making her jump, and Alice turned sharply to see Felicity standing there.

'Sorry, I didn't mean to frighten you,' said Felicity. 'The thing is, Alice, I heard what you said to young Violet just then. I had no intention of listening in, but I was just coming round the corner, so I couldn't help it.'

'Oh!' said Alice, looking rather alarmed. 'Do you think that I shouldn't have said anything?'

'Not at all,' said Felicity emphatically. 'As top formers, it is our job to guide and advise the young ones, and what you said was fine. I couldn't have put it better myself.'

Alice felt so thrilled that she was quite speechless for a moment, and Felicity went on, 'You sounded as though you were speaking from experience.'

'Violet reminds me of – of someone I used to know,' said Alice. 'This girl made herself very unpopular indeed, and I shouldn't like to see Violet going the same way.'

'Well, you've certainly done all you can to put her on the right track,' said Felicity, taking the girl's arm as the two of them began to walk towards the school. She felt pleased to have discovered that Alice had another side to her personality, and there was more to her than the timid, eager-to-please girl the sixth formers knew. But there was still such a lot about her that they had yet to discover, and Felicity decided to ask the girl a question that had been on her mind.

'Alice,' she said, pulling the girl to a halt suddenly. 'Why is it that you are so determined to go out of your way to run errands for others, and make a slave of yourself for someone like Amy?'

The ready colour rushed to Alice's cheeks again, her tone a little breathless as she said, 'It's quite simple. I just like to help people. I know that I am privileged in some ways, and this is my way of giving back. It's as Miss

Grayling said in her speech, on the first day of term – *You will all get a lot out of your time at Malory Towers. See that you put a lot back.*'

'Yes, I see,' said Felicity, thinking that Amy had been right, and that Alice must come from a very wealthy family indeed, if she felt the need to give so much back. But something about the girl's words troubled her, something that she couldn't quite put her finger on.

It was as Felicity was dropping off to sleep that night that she realised what it was, and the thought made her wide awake.

Alice had quoted words to her that Miss Grayling was supposed to have said in her speech. But Felicity had been outside the door, listening, and the Head *hadn't* said those words, although she usually included them. But this time, the telephone had rung before she was able to say the words. So where had Alice heard them?

Daffy is deceitful

There was a slight chill in the air on the morning of the first formers' picnic, but it was bright and sunny, with no wind, and nothing could mar their high spirits.

'We're setting off shortly before noon, aren't we?' said Katie. 'It should be a bit warmer by then.'

'We're to go to the kitchen later, to help Cook cut sandwiches to take with us,' said Daffy.

'And I must pop to the baker's, to collect my cake,' said Violet, with a great air of self-importance.

'Well, you can't go alone,' said Faith. 'Only the fifth and sixth formers are allowed out on their own. Someone must go with you.'

Unsurprisingly, no one was keen on the idea of walking to the baker's shop with Violet and, in the end, Faith, as head-girl, decided that she had better volunteer herself.

'Don't be long!' Daffy called after them. 'We shall need everyone to pitch in and help with the sandwiches.'

'Yes, Daffy,' said Faith meekly and, casting a sidelong glance at her, Violet wondered how the quiet, timid head-girl felt about Daffy usurping her authority and taking over as leader of the first form. Faith had no special friend of her own, and never confided in anyone, and Violet thought that she might be glad of someone to talk to. Why, for all she knew, the head-girl might feel just as bitter towards Daffy as she, Violet, did, and it would be good to have someone on her side.

So, as the two girls walked, Violet was at her sweetest, taking great pains to encourage Faith to talk.

Used to being overlooked by the others, Faith wasn't accustomed to talking about herself and was a little reticent at first. But she soon blossomed under Violet's interest, and began telling the girl all about her parents, and her two young brothers. Of course, all of this was very boring to the self-centred Violet, but she put up with it patiently, just waiting for a chance to drop Daffy's name into the conversation.

And Violet's patience was rewarded, for as they left the baker's shop with the chocolate cake, all neatly wrapped in a cardboard box, done up with string, they bumped into Gillian and Delia.

'Hallo, kids!' said Gillian. 'That's a most interesting-looking box you have there, young Violet.'

'It's a chocolate cake, Gillian,' said Violet. 'For our picnic later.'

'Oh yes, you first formers are all going to the beach, aren't you?' said Delia. 'Well, not quite all of you, for, of course, Daffy Hope will be left behind.'

'Serves her right, if you ask me,' said Gillian. 'She's not a bad kid, but that was a very dangerous trick she played on you the other day, Violet. I think that Felicity's punishment of not allowing her to go to the picnic was very just.'.

Of course, this was news to the two first formers, who both looked quite astonished. Violet recovered quickly, however, and said graciously, 'Well, I was very upset and frightened, but I do feel sorry for Daffy, being left behind. I shall have to save her a piece of my chocolate cake.'

Faith, not quite as quick-brained or as cunning as Violet, listened to all this with a puzzled frown on her face, and, seeing that she was about to seek enlightenment from the two sixth formers, Violet seized her arm, saying, 'Well, I suppose that we had better hurry back to school, or the others will think that we have got lost. Goodbye, Gillian. Goodbye, Delia.'

And, carrying the cake-box between them, the two first formers began to make their way back to school. Once they were out of earshot of the sixth formers, Faith stopped, and said, 'Well, what do you make of that, Violet? I could have sworn that Daffy told us Felicity had let her off without a punishment.'

'She did tell us that,' said Violet with a snort. 'Because she wanted us to think that she is well in with the Head Girl. But now we know the truth – Felicity forbade Daffy to take part in the picnic, and Daffy intends to disobey her.'

'Oh dear!' wailed Faith. 'It really is terribly wrong of Daffy, and I know that it's my place to tell her that she is in the wrong, and shouldn't come on the picnic. But Daffy is a strong character, and I am not! Violet, how on earth am I to get her to listen to me?'

Violet's mind had been working quickly, and she said, 'Well, I don't see how you can be held responsible if Daffy chooses to be naughty and disobedient. I think that you should tell her that you know the truth, and what she decides to do after that is really a matter for her and her conscience.'

'I suppose that you are right,' sighed Faith. 'I only hope that Felicity doesn't find out, or Daffy *will* be in hot water.'

Violet smiled to herself at this. Felicity *was* going to find out – she would make sure of that!

'I do admire your patience, Faith,' said Violet sweetly. 'It must be so irritating for you when Daffy tries to take the lead all the time, when it should be you who does so.'

'I'm not cut out to be head-girl, I know that, for I am not a leader,' said Faith, sounding unhappy. 'Miss Potts only allowed me to be because I had already been in the first form for one term.'

'Well, it's early days yet,' said Violet. 'There is plenty of time for you to learn how to become a good head-girl. And how to put that dreadful Daffy in her place!'

Faith looked so alarmed at the thought of putting Daffy in her place that Violet decided she had better change the subject. She chatted amicably to the girl as they walked back to school, telling Faith all about her doting parents, her beautiful home and her beloved Siamese cat, Willow.

Faith, like the rest of her form, thought that Violet was boastful and rather snobbish, but found herself warming to the girl. So few of the first formers took the trouble to talk to her, that it was rather pleasant to enjoy a gossip like this – even though Violet was doing most of the talking!

As they reached the school gates, Violet said, 'You know, Faith, I really have enjoyed your company this morning. Now, I know that you don't have a particular friend, and nor do I, so what do you say to the two of us palling up?'

Faith didn't know quite *what* to say. This was the first time that anyone had asked to be her friend, and her heart was warmed. But the other girls wouldn't like it at all, and might shun her as they shunned Violet.

Violet wasn't particularly clever, but she could be quite sly and cunning when she set her mind to something, and she guessed at the thoughts that were running through Faith's head.

'Of course, I shall quite understand if you don't want to be friends,' she said, sounding rather forlorn. 'I know that the others don't like me very much. But then, they don't seem to have an awful lot of time for you either, probably because you are so quiet. It just seems a shame that we should both be on our own, when we could have so much fun together.'

Violet's words tipped the scales and, from somewhere inside herself, Faith found a spark of courage. Why should she let Daffy, Katie and the rest of them stop her from making a friend, when none of them wanted to befriend her themselves? Let them think what they wanted to!

'You're quite right,' she said, smiling shyly at Violet. 'I should like to be friends with you very much.'

So when the two girls joined the others in the kitchen to help cut sandwiches, the rest of the first formers were astonished to see them giggling and chattering away together as they worked.

'I'm surprised at you, Faith,' said Daffy, finding herself next to the head-girl as the two of them washed up afterwards. 'I thought you had more sense than to make friends with Her Highness.'

Faith was needled by this and, though her voice trembled a little at her own daring, she managed to retort, 'And *I'm* surprised at *you*, Daffy. For I know that Felicity told you you were not to join us on the picnic. It really is very deceitful of you to disobey her, you know.'

Daffy was so taken aback at these harsh words from the timid Faith that she completely forgot to ask the girl how she knew all this. And – most unusually for Daffy – she was quite speechless for a moment.

She soon found her tongue, however, and said, 'You're not going to sneak on me, are you?'

'Of course not!' said Faith indignantly. 'Why, I would never do such a thing! Though I should think more of you, Daffy, if you showed a little respect for Felicity and did as she told you.'

But Daffy didn't care very much for Faith's opinion of her, and was determined to go on the picnic with the others.

Meanwhile, Violet, busy packing one of the picnic baskets that the first formers were taking with them, was thinking hard. How could she make sure that Daffy was found out by Felicity? Sneaking was quite out of the question, for Felicity would be so disgusted with Violet that she might even refuse to listen to her. Besides, Violet didn't want to come out into the open, or Felicity might let Daffy know who was responsible for her disgrace. What about an anonymous letter, slipped under the door of the Head Girl's study?

No, that was no good either, for it could easily be dismissed as a piece of spite, or an attempt at stirring up trouble. What Violet needed was something that would prove, beyond doubt, that Daffy had been to the picnic.

Suddenly an idea came to her, and she darted towards the kitchen door, Ivy calling after her, 'I say, Violet, where are you going? We shall be leaving in a few minutes!'

'I just need to fetch something from the dormitory,' Violet called back. 'I shall be back in two ticks.'

So she was. Most of the others had gone on ahead, but Faith had hung back, waiting for Violet.

'What's that?' she asked, noticing that Violet had a small bag slung over her shoulder.

'My camera,' said Violet. 'It was a birthday gift from my uncle, and it's a really good one. I thought that it might be nice to take some photographs at the picnic, and put them in an album.'

'What a super idea,' said Faith. 'It will be something nice to look back on when we are top formers.'

Violet agreed to this with a smile. Little did Faith realise that she had quite different plans for the photographs! She badly wanted to get her own back on Daffy, for it was all her fault that she now had to take swimming lessons from June. How she hated having to bathe in that beastly, cold water! And how she hated June and her sharp tongue, though she would never dare say so to the girl's face! Violet was the only girl in the school who was hoping that the spell of unseasonably mild weather would break, for once it did she would be safe from swimming lessons until the spring.

Felicity and Susan, meanwhile, had popped down to the stables with Julie and Lucy.

'I've hardly seen anything of Jack and Sandy this term,' said Felicity. 'And I've been saving some sugar lumps for them both. Hallo, who's this?'

A little tabby cat was sitting outside Jack's stable, and as the four girls approached she padded towards them, mewing in greeting.

'This is Queenie,' said Lucy with a grin. 'She belongs to one of the gardeners, and Miss Grayling has given permission for her to live in the stables.'

'She's awfully sweet,' said Susan, bending to stroke the little cat, who purred in appreciation. 'Reminds me a bit of our cat at home.'

'Jack and Sandy simply adore her,' said Lucy. 'Just watch this.'

Lucy opened the door of Sandy's stable, and the cat darted in, going straight up to the horse and weaving in and out of his legs, purring ever more loudly. Sandy wasn't at all alarmed, but whinnied softly, as if he were greeting his little friend, before bending his head and nudging Queenie gently with his big muzzle.

'Well, Sandy, it looks as if you have another admirer,' said Felicity, patting the horse's sleek neck. 'It's a wonder that you and Jack don't get quite big-headed, with all the fuss that is made of you both.'

In the end, Felicity and Susan decided to accompany the other two girls over to Five Oaks, the local riding stables. Five Oaks was run by two old Malory Towers girls, Bill and Clarissa, and the sixth formers often popped in to visit them.

Julie and Lucy went on horseback, of course, while Felicity and Susan had to walk, and the girls were most amused when Queenie attempted to follow them out of the stable yard.

'No, Queenie, I'm afraid that you can't come with us,' said Susan with a laugh. 'You might wander off and get lost.'

Fortunately, the gardener who owned Queenie appeared then, with her dinner, so the cat was distracted and the girls made their escape.

The four spent a pleasant afternoon at Five Oaks, Julie and Lucy enjoying a canter round the paddock, while Felicity and Susan petted the horses and strolled about the grounds. Then they sat in Bill and Clarissa's cosy kitchen, chatting with the two girls as they ate slices of Clarissa's delicious home-made fruit cake, washed down with big cups of tea. Bill was just about to refill their cups when a distant, ominous rumble could be heard, and Lucy said in dismay, 'Oh dear, surely that can't be thunder?'

'I'm afraid that it is,' said Clarissa, who had got up to peer out of the window. 'The sky has suddenly gone awfully grey.'

'We had better get the horses back to school, in that case,' said Julie. 'Poor Jack doesn't like storms at all, and I'd like to stable him before it breaks.'

Fortunately it was only a five-minute ride from Five Oaks to Malory Towers, but it took Felicity and Susan, on foot, a little longer. By the time that they reached the school gates, Julie and Lucy were already stabling their horses, and big drops of rain had just started to fall.

'Phew!' said Susan. 'It looks as if we got back just in time.'

'We are not the only ones,' said Felicity, nodding towards a group of girls who were approaching the gates from the other direction. 'It's the first formers coming back from their picnic.'

The first formers had had a simply marvellous time, making sandcastles, taking their shoes and socks off and paddling at the water's edge, and, of course, eating the delicious picnic.

Violet cut everyone an enormous slice of her chocolate cake, which everyone agreed was simply scrumptious.

'The best cake I've ever tasted.'

'Heavenly! It just melts in the mouth.'

'Delicious! Thanks very much, Violet.'

Daffy and one or two others waited for Violet to boast about how much the cake had cost, but, to their surprise, she accepted everyone's thanks and compliments with a smile. The girl really was on her best behaviour, Daffy realised, when she got out her camera and said cheerily, 'Let's take some photographs so that we can all remember this happy time.'

'Ooh, yes, let's!' cried Katie, clapping her hands together. 'Violet, will you take one of Daffy and me, please?'

Of course, Violet was only too happy to do this, and it didn't occur to Daffy for a second that allowing herself to be photographed at the picnic was rather foolish. The girls posed happily, pulling silly faces at the camera, and Daffy was silliest of all, getting herself into almost every photograph. At last, Violet said, 'That's it, I'm afraid. The film is all used up now. Faith, if you will come into town with me on Monday I can take it in to be developed.'

'Of course,' said Faith at once. 'I can't wait to see them.'

And that was when the sky had turned dark, and the same rumble of thunder that the girls at Five Oaks had heard sounded. Some of the girls were scared of thunder, and they began packing everything away rapidly.

'We had better get back to school before the heavens open,' said Ivy with a shiver. 'Come along, everyone!'

The girls trooped happily back to school, and it was as they were almost at the gates that they saw Felicity and Susan coming towards them.

Daffy was at the back of the little group, and she cast a horrified glance at Katie, who acted quickly.

'Get behind that tree,' she hissed, giving her friend a shove. 'And don't move until you're certain Felicity and Susan have gone.'

The two sixth formers greeted the first formers as they turned in at the gates together, Felicity swiftly running an eye over the group to make sure that Daffy wasn't there. She felt pleased when she realised that the girl had obeyed her orders, and hoped that she wouldn't have reason to punish the first former again.

There was no time to ask the youngsters how they had enjoyed their picnic, for just then the heavens *did* open, and the first formers ran squealing towards the school.

Felicity and Susan followed in a more orderly fashion, and soon only Daffy was left outside in the rain. The girl waited for a few moments before stepping out from the shelter of the tree, then she moved stealthily up to the gates, slipping through them when she realised that the others were out of sight. Walking up the long drive, the girl grinned to herself. She had got away with it!

A marvellous trick

'My word, won't I be glad when Higher Cert is behind us and we can relax a little,' said Felicity to Susan as the two girls slipped into their seats in the class-room. 'Thank heavens we don't have Maths this morning, for I spent all of last night studying it and I simply couldn't face it today.'

'Well, it won't be long now,' said Susan. 'Only a couple of weeks until half-term, and the exams start immediately afterwards.'

'And once the exams have finished, we have our lacrosse matches against Marlowe Hall,' said June. 'It's a pity that you two are so busy studying that you haven't had much time to practice, otherwise I should certainly have put you in the upper-school team. As it is, I have had to fall back on the fourth and fifth formers.'

'You will be in the team though, won't you, June?' said Felicity. 'We must have *someone* from the sixth on there.'

'Oh yes, I shall be playing all right,' said June, who didn't seem to be feeling the pressure of the forthcoming exams as the others did.

'Lucky you,' said Susan enviously. 'I wish that I

had your marvellous memory and didn't need to study so hard.'

'Yes, it's awfully unfair,' said Freddie, joining in. 'While I'm sighing and groaning over my books for hours, June has memorised everything in a matter of minutes and is off to lacrosse practice.'

'I'm just lucky, I suppose,' said June. 'It must run in the family, for my cousin, Alicia, was just the same.'

'I wish it ran in my family,' sighed Felicity. 'But I know that Darrell had to study just as hard as me to get good results.'

'Well, I'm just as busy as you are, in my own way,' said June. 'What with arranging practice times and coaching. Thank goodness the weather has turned too cold for swimming now, and I don't have to give Violet swimming lessons any more. I don't know who found them more trying, her or me!'

Then the girls fell silent, getting to their feet as they heard Miss Oakes approaching, and soon the English lesson was under way, the sixth formers silent as they concentrated hard on their work.

Miss Oakes, looking at all the heads bent over books, felt very pleased with her form, for the majority of them were good, hard-working girls. The mistress knew very well that, if she were to leave the room now, they could be trusted to get on with their work and not play the fool. Even June, who had been such a scamp when she was lower down in the school!

The first formers, however, in the class-room next to

the sixth form's, could *not* be trusted alone, and they were very pleased that Mam'zelle Dupont was late, for they were planning a little surprise for her!

The first form had an extra member that morning – in the form of Queenie, the stable cat. The girls had taken her from the stables after breakfast, and had been playing with her non-stop, so that now the little creature was ready for a nap.

'Which is just what we want,' said Daffy happily, stroking Queenie as she lay peacefully on her lap. 'We don't want the cat getting out of the bag too soon!'

'We had better hide her quickly,' said Katie. 'Mam'zelle could arrive at any second.'

Daffy gently lifted the cat up, and gave her to a girl called Jenny, who sat at the front of the class.

'You know what you have to do, Jenny,' said Daffy.

Jenny, her eyes alight with amusement, nodded eagerly as she took Queenie, placing the sleeping cat on the floor between her desk and Violet's.

'Move your satchel, Violet,' said Jenny. 'And I'll put mine just here, so that Mam'zelle won't be able to see Queenie from her desk.'

Violet obliged, for she was looking forward to the trick as much as the others. She was very poor at French, and had come in for a great many scoldings from Mam'zelle, so anything that wasted time in the class was fine by her.

She didn't care for Queenie, however, and said with a sniff, 'How very ordinary she looks, compared to my own beautiful Willow. Willow has the most wonderful blue eyes, and she wears a collar set with tiny little jewels, and –'

'And she eats fresh salmon every day, out of a dish made from the finest bone china,' said Daffy, making the others laugh.

Violet scowled, but there was no time to retort, for the sound of Mam'zelle Dupont's high heels could be heard coming along the corridor, and Daffy rushed to hold the door open for her.

Mam'zelle looked flustered, for she hated being late for any class, but Daffy had quickly become one of her favourites, and the sight of the girl's sweet smile soothed her a little.

'*Merci*, Daphne,' she said, patting the girl's dark curls, before walking to the big desk at the front of the class. '*Bonjour, mes enfants*. Sit down, please, and get out the French grammar prep that I set you on Monday.'

The girls got their books from their desks, and Daffy put up her hand, saying, 'Please, Mam'zelle, I have done my very best, but I'm afraid that I didn't understand some of the grammar rules that you explained to us. Would you mind awfully explaining to me again, for I do so want to do well at French?'

Of course, Mam'zelle was delighted to hear this, and only too happy to help her favourite, and she went to Daffy's side at once. The girl's desk was at the back of the classroom and, as soon as the French mistress's back was turned, Jenny moved swiftly.

Mam'zelle Dupont had a very large handbag, which she took everywhere with her, and it sat unattended under her desk now. Quickly, Jenny scooped up Queenie, carried her to the mistress's desk, and deposited her in the handbag. The cat, annoyed at having her nap disturbed, opened her eyes and gave a little mew of protest, but fortunately Ivy happened to sneeze loudly at the same time, so Mam'zelle heard nothing. Once she was in the bag, which was warm and comfortable, Queenie soon settled down again and, with one eye on Mam'zelle, Jenny fastened the top of the bag, leaving a little gap so that the cat could breathe.

Then she darted back to her seat, winking at the others, who were all doing their utmost to stifle their giggles.

At last Mam'zelle finished with Daffy, then she went round the class collecting everyone's prep, before returning to her own desk. The lesson progressed smoothly, until Queenie, refreshed by her long nap, awoke, feeling in need of a little exercise.

Mam'zelle was writing something on the blackboard when she became aware of a strange noise coming from under her desk, and she turned sharply.

'*Tiens!*' cried the French mistress, looking most alarmed. 'What is this strange noise that comes from under my desk?'

'A strange noise, Mam'zelle?' said Jenny, looking puzzled. 'I can't hear anything. Can you, Violet?'

Violet shook her head solemnly, and just then the noise started again, more loudly this time. It really was a most peculiar sound, thought Mam'zelle, a strange hissing and spitting and yowling, as though some wild beast was under her desk, but there was nothing to be seen.

Of course, all of the girls could hear the noise, and all of them were struggling to contain their laughter now. Katie had stuffed a handkerchief into her mouth, while Ivy lifted the lid of her desk to hide her mirth from the French mistress.

Then Mam'zelle gave a little shriek, tottering backwards on the high-heeled shoes she always wore, and Daffy said, 'Why, Mam'zelle, whatever is the matter?'

'My bag, he moved!' wailed poor Mam'zelle, as white as a sheet. 'He wobbled from side to side, then jumped up and down.'

'But that's impossible!' said Daffy, making a tremendous effort to keep her face straight.

'Ah, Daphne, it is not impossible, for it is happening!' cried Mam'zelle. 'Come and see for yourself, then you shall believe me.'

Mam'zelle meant for Daffy to come and see, but the whole class surged forward, crowding around Mam'zelle's desk.

'I can hear something!' said Katie. 'And it seems to be coming from your handbag, Mam'zelle.'

'I hear it too,' said Daffy gravely. 'It sounds like – like a soul in torment!'

'Nonsense!' said Mam'zelle stoutly, though she looked a little alarmed. 'I have no tormented souls in my handbag.'

This was too much for Ivy, who went off into a peal of laughter, so contagious that several of the others joined in. Katie was holding her sides, while tears poured down Faith's cheeks.

'Ah, *méchantes filles*!' cried Mam'zelle. 'I do not see anything at all amusing about this.'

'Mam'zelle, I really think that you should open your handbag, so that you can see exactly what is going on in there,' said Jenny.

Mam'zelle gave a little moan and seemed rooted to the spot. It was quite plain that she was far too afraid to open the bag, and Daffy stepped forward, saying nobly, 'Mam'zelle, with your permission, *I* shall open the bag. Please stand back, everyone.'

Mam'zelle jumped back at once, almost treading on Violet's toes, and the girls, giggling, followed suit.

Cautiously, her expression very grave indeed, Daffy moved towards the handbag and unfastened it, making it look as though her hands were shaking uncontrollably, so that the others started to laugh again. Then she pulled the handbag open, springing to her feet and giving a squeal as Queenie shot out. Mam'zelle was no great lover of cats, and she, too, squealed as Queenie made straight for her, while the first formers roared with laughter.

In the class-room next door, Miss Oakes and the sixth formers wondered what on earth was going on.

The first formers had been noisy all morning, and Miss Oakes had cast a great many irritated glares at the wall that separated the two class-rooms. Now, though, it sounded as though a perfect riot was going on, making it quite impossible for the sixth formers to concentrate. Miss Oakes gave an angry exclamation as she stalked to the door. It seemed that Mam'zelle must have left the room, and those irresponsible first formers had taken advantage of her absence to act the goat. Well, Miss Oakes would soon set them straight!

The mistress got the shock of her life when she pushed open the door of the first-form class-room and a little tabby cat shot out straight past her, then ran away down the corridor as if her life depended on it.

And, far from being away from the class, Mam'zelle Dupont was in the thick of the disturbance. She sat in her chair now, as white as a sheet, while Daffy fanned her with a book and the rest of the first form stood around, chattering excitedly.

'Mam'zelle!' said the mistress sharply. 'What on earth is going on here? My girls can hardly hear themselves think!'

Miss Oakes's stern tone quelled the first formers, who all slunk away to their seats, and Mam'zelle sat up straight in her chair and said excitably, 'Ah, Miss Oakes, it was dreadful. The cat was in my bag, and then she got out of the bag and attacked me!'

Of course, poor Queenie hadn't attacked Mam'zelle at all. The little cat was very affectionate, and had simply rubbed herself against Mam'zelle's legs. Mam'zelle, however, had not appreciated this gesture at all, and, for one moment, the girls had thought she was about to faint.

'A cat in your bag, Mam'zelle?' repeated the astonished Miss Oakes. 'How did a cat come to be in your bag, may I ask?'

Mam'zelle Dupont had been so bewildered by the morning's happenings that she hadn't had leisure to consider this. Now, though, a doubtful look came across her face and she looked suspiciously at the first formers. Each and every one of them, though, looked a picture of innocence, and Mam'zelle dismissed her unworthy suspicions at once.

'It is a mystery,' she said to Miss Oakes. 'It must have climbed in and gone to sleep while my bag was open.'

'Hmm,' said the sixth-form mistress, also looking at the innocent faces of the first formers. Miss Oakes was not so easily fooled as Mam'zelle, and she wasn't taken in for one moment.

'Well, I shall leave you to it, Mam'zelle,' she said. 'And I trust that I shan't have cause to come in and complain again!'

Mam'zelle felt rather put out at being spoken to in such a way. Ah, how hard and unfeeling these English mistresses could be at times, to those of a more sensitive disposition. Miss Oakes had seen how distressed she, Mam'zelle, was, yet had not spoken one word of comfort.

But the girls could see that Mam'zelle was 'in a paddy', as Daffy put it, and were at their sweetest, sympathising warmly with the French mistress as she speculated on how Queenie could have come to be in her bag, and talked at length about her dislike of cats. In fact, Mam'zelle talked so much that she wasted the rest of the lesson, just as the naughty first formers had hoped! But the first formers had gone up in her estimation, for they were dear, good-hearted girls and their concern for her had warmed her heart.

'Dear old Mam'zelle,' chuckled Ivy, as the class followed the French mistress along the corridor. 'She doesn't so much as suspect that we were the ones who put Queenie in her bag.'

'My big sister, Sally, told me that she was a most marvellous person to play tricks on,' said Daffy with satisfaction. 'And it seems that she was right.'

'Was Sally as naughty and daring as you are, Daffy?' asked Jenny curiously.

'Heavens, no!' said Daffy, with a giggle. 'She was as good as gold. I mean to say, she enjoyed a joke and a trick, but she was more of a watcher than a doer.'

'And you are most definitely a doer, Daffy!' giggled Katie. 'I say, did Sally give you any useful information on the other mistresses?'

'A little,' answered Daffy. 'She warned me to beware of Mam'zelle Rougier's temper, and not to get on the wrong side of Miss Potts.'

'She's quite right,' said Faith seriously. 'Don't forget that I have already been in her form for one term, and I know how stern she can be at times.'

'She's not a bad sort,' said Ivy. 'Although I certainly

wouldn't like to be in her bad books.'

'Yes, you had better watch out, Daffy,' said Maggie. 'Potty looked at you most suspiciously the other day, when she was talking about the tricks that had been played on Violet.'

But Daffy only laughed, saying with a careless shrug, 'I'm not afraid of old Potty. She might be sharp, but I've never met a mistress who can get the better of me!'

Puzzles and plots

As it was the largest, Felicity's study soon became a meeting place for the North Tower sixth formers. At a pinch, they could all squeeze in, though it meant girls sitting on the desk and window-sill, or even on the floor!

Felicity was quite happy for her study to be used as a common-room some of the time, provided that the others understood that there were times when she needed to study and must not be disturbed.

But, although the sixth formers knew this, the younger girls didn't, and Felicity often *was* disturbed, by a timid tapping on the door, as one member or other of the lower forms asked her advice on a problem. However busy she was, Felicity never turned anyone away, for it was her duty to help and guide the youngsters, and one she was determined not to shirk.

June also had a devoted following of youngsters, and one person who looked up to her enormously was Daffy Hope.

Daffy had heard all about June from her sister, Sally, long before she had started at Malory Towers. June, according to Sally, was the wickedest, boldest girl that the school had ever had, famed for her ready wit, sharp tongue and – above all – her jokes and tricks. Daffy longed to be just like her and, although June had not put her in the lacrosse team, the girl looked up to her no end.

She was delighted when, the day after the trick on Mam'zelle, June had stopped her in the corridor, and said, in a low voice, 'What's all this I hear about the stable cat getting into Mam'zelle Dupont's handbag?'

For a moment Daffy had wondered if she was in for a scold, then she saw the twinkle in June's eyes and grinned, saying innocently, 'That was quite a mystery, June. I simply can't imagine how the poor creature came to be trapped in there.'

June laughed out loud at this, and said, 'You're a monkey, Daffy Hope! Well, it's good to know that there is someone who will keep the tradition of playing tricks going at Malory Towers once I have left. Keep up the good work!'

Daffy, of course, had seen this as praise of the highest order, and walked off with her head in such a whirl that she almost bumped into Mam'zelle Rougier.

'Oops, sorry, Mam'zelle!' she said. 'I didn't see you there.'

The thin, rather severe-looking French mistress glared at Daffy, and shook her head sternly, but the first former didn't even notice. What did anything matter, when she was basking in the glow of June's praise? And it was much more pleasant to be praised for jokes and tricks than for her skill at games, Daffy thought. After all, there were many good lacrosse players at Malory Towers, but there was no one who could plan a successful trick like she, Daffy, could.

June, meanwhile, went off to join a little gathering in Felicity's study. Susan was there, of course, along with Bonnie, Amy, Delia and Gillian, all of them drinking cups of tea and happily munching on biscuits.

'Room for one more?' asked June, sidling in.

'Yes, but I'm afraid you'll have to sit on the floor,' said Felicity. 'Do help yourself to tea and biscuits.'

June did so, then found herself a comfortable spot on the floor, her back resting against the wall.

The sixth formers chattered amicably about anything and everything – except the forthcoming exams. It had been agreed that, when they all got together like this, the subject was out of bounds, and was only ever mentioned in passing. If anyone ever tried to discuss the exams in any depth, they were immediately shouted down and threatened with being sent from the room!

'Yes, it's bad enough that we have to do all this studying,' Gillian had said. 'When we get the chance to meet up in what little free time we have, we need to put them out of our minds completely.'

'Half-term soon,' said Susan, taking a bite of a ginger biscuit. 'Goodness, haven't the weeks just flown!'

'I'll say,' said Delia. 'I simply can't tell you how much I'm looking forward to seeing my father.'

All of the girls were looking forward to seeing their people again, and Felicity said, 'No matter how far up the school you get, the excitement of half-term never fades.'

Alice put her head round the door just then, and, seeing that the room was so crowded, she said, 'Oh! Sorry, Felicity, I didn't realise that so many of the girls were in here. I'll come back another time.'

'No, come in, Alice,' called Susan in a cheery voice. 'Felicity doesn't mind her study being used as a meeting place at all!'

So Alice squeezed in, poured herself a cup of tea and sat down next to June.

'We were just talking about half-term, Alice,' said June. 'Will your parents be coming?'

'Oh, no!' said Alice, looking quite horrified at the thought.

This puzzled the others and, seeing their expressions, Alice said hastily, 'They will be on holiday, you see. It was all arranged ages ago, so they can't cancel now.'

'What a shame,' said Felicity, feeling sorry for the girl. 'Well, you're very welcome to come out with me and my people, you know. I'm not sure whether they'll be bringing a picnic, or taking me to a restaurant, but it's sure to be good fun.'

'Why, thank you, Felicity,' said Alice, her face lighting up. 'I would like that very much.'

Delia and Gillian got up to leave, and June moved over to sit in the empty chair beside Felicity, murmuring, 'Rather you than me.'

'Oh, June, that's a little unkind!' protested Felicity. 'Alice might be a little odd, but she's not a bad sort.'

As she spoke, a memory of something that Alice

had said to her the other day came back to Felicity. She had meant to question Alice about it, but had been so busy that it had slipped to the back of her mind. She mentioned it now to June, saying in a low voice, 'June, you know on the first day of term I took the new girls to see Miss Grayling?'

June nodded, and Felicity went on, 'Well, Alice said to me the other day that the Head had said to them, *You will all get a lot out of your time at Malory Towers. Make sure that you put a lot back.*'

June shrugged, and said, 'Miss Grayling always says that to the new girls on their first day. I can remember her saying it to us.'

'But that's just it,' said Felicity. 'She *didn't* say it this time! The telephone in her study rang just as she was about to get to that bit. I was outside and heard everything quite clearly.'

'That *is* peculiar,' said June. 'Have you tackled Alice about it?'

'No, I meant to, but with one thing and another it sort of slipped my mind,' said Felicity.

'Do it now,' said June.

'No, not with so many people around,' said Felicity firmly. 'I shall speak to her about it when we are alone.'

Both girls glanced across at Alice, who had taken her glasses off and was rubbing at her eyes.

'It's very strange,' said June. 'But it's only at certain times I get that feeling of familiarity about Alice. And this is one of those times.'

'It's because she's taken her glasses off,' said Felicity. 'I always get it then as well. And when she smiles.'

June made no reply, for she was staring at Alice hard. Felicity gave her a nudge, saying, 'What's up with you? I thought you said that the only reason Alice seems familiar is because she reminds us of someone.'

'I did,' said June, bringing her gaze back to Felicity. 'But now I'm having second thoughts. After what you have just told me, I'm beginning to think that there is a decided mystery about our Alice. And did you notice how she reacted when I asked if her people were coming at half-term?'

'Yes,' said Felicity. 'Almost as if she was ashamed of them.'

'Or terrified of us meeting them,' said June. 'I think that once the exams are over, we might do a little investigating.'

'Yes,' said Felicity, nodding. 'My word, I was hoping for an easy time after the exams, but what with trying to find out what's up with Alice – not to mention stopping her running round after Amy – I'm going to have my hands full!'

Soon after that, the group began to break up, until only Felicity, June and Bonnie were left.

'I suppose I had better leave, too,' said Bonnie, getting up and moving to the door.

'Stop a minute, Bonnie!' Felicity called out, suddenly spotting something. 'Alice has left her glasses on the floor, and you almost stepped on them.'

Bonnie glanced down at the floor, picking up a pair of glasses that lay near her feet.

'How careless of her!' she exclaimed. 'I say, shall I try them on?'

And, without waiting for an answer, Bonnie slipped the glasses on to her nose, much to the amusement of the other two.

'My goodness, you do look different, Bonnie!' laughed June. 'Very sober and studious!'

'Yes,' said Felicity, grinning. 'It's amazing the difference that a pair of glasses can make to a face. But you'd better take them back to Alice, Bonnie. I bet she's as blind as a bat without them.'

'And I'll bet she isn't,' said Bonnie in rather an odd voice, taking the glasses off and looking at them with a puzzled expression.

'Why do you say that?' asked June, frowning.

'Because the lenses are made from plain glass,' said Bonnie.

'Are you quite sure?' asked June, astonished.

'See for yourself,' said Bonnie, handing the glasses to June.

The girl put them on, exclaiming, 'Bonnie is right! But why on earth would Alice wear glasses made from plain glass?'

'It makes no sense at all,' said Felicity, completely bewildered.

'There are quite a few things about Alice that don't make sense,' said June, giving the glasses back to Bonnie.

'She is hiding something, I'm sure of it, and it must be something bad.'

'You can't be certain of that, June,' protested Felicity, who didn't see things in quite such a black and white way as the other girl.

'I can,' replied June. 'Otherwise why would she bother to hide it at all?'

Felicity couldn't think of an answer to this, except that she felt, instinctively, that Alice wasn't a bad person.

'What do you think, Bonnie?' she asked.

'I don't know *what* to think,' said Bonnie. 'But I can tell you one thing.'

'What?' chorused Felicity and June.

'She hasn't been wearing glasses for long,' said Bonnie. 'You see, people who have been wearing glasses for a long time get little dents either side of the bridge of their nose. My aunts have them, and so does my cousin. Alice doesn't. I noticed that the other night, when she took them off to go to bed.'

'Yes, you're right!' exclaimed June. 'My father and grandparents have them too.'

'Well, I'll take them across to Alice now,' said Bonnie. 'Do you want me to say anything to her?'

June and Felicity exchanged glances, then Felicity said, 'No, not yet. I think that Alice has something to hide, just as you do, June, though I don't necessarily think it's something bad. But until we are certain, and have time to get to the bottom of things properly, I would rather not put her on her guard.'

As Bonnie left, June said to Felicity, 'I bet you regret asking her out with you and your people at half-term now.'

'No,' said Felicity, after considering this for a moment. 'If she is having a happy time and feeling relaxed, she may let something slip.'

'Yes, you may be right,' said June. Then she looked at her watch, saying, 'Heavens, I've got lacrosse practice with the lower school in five minutes! I'll just go and round up Freddie. Would you like to come along with us, Felicity, and give your expert opinion?'

'I don't know about my opinion being *expert* exactly!' laughed Felicity. 'And I really should get down to some studying. But it's awfully tempting to play truant for an hour or two, and see how the kids are doing.'

'Marvellous!' said June, grinning as she hauled Felicity to her feet. 'Come along then, let's go and find old Freddie!'

The weather was a little chilly that afternoon, and the three sixth formers wrapped up warmly in coats, hats and scarves as they stood watching the first and second formers play lacrosse.

'Well played, Hilda!' yelled June. 'Maggie, stick closer to Elizabeth – yes, that's it!'

'Young Daffy Hope plays jolly well,' said Felicity, watching the girl as she ran down the field like a streak of lightning. 'Yet I notice that you haven't put her in the team, June.'

'She's marvellous,' agreed June. 'When she wants to

be. But, at any second, she could lose interest in the game and start playing the fool to amuse her friends.'

'Can't afford to have anyone with that attitude on the team,' said Freddie. 'Imagine if she did that in a match!'

But, for once, Daffy *didn't* play the fool. She wanted to show June that she had made a big mistake in leaving her out of the team, so the girl put every ounce of effort into the game and played superbly.

June noticed, and was impressed. As the game ended, she murmured to Felicity and Freddie, 'Well, it looks as though I may have to eat my words. Daffy, come here!'

Daffy walked across to June, and the games captain took her to one side, saying, 'Look here, Daffy, you did jolly well today. Turning over a new leaf?'

'I am as far as lacrosse is concerned,' answered Daffy.

'Well, what a pity that it's too late to put you in the team now,' said June. 'Now that the players have been announced, it really wouldn't be fair of me to drop one of the others to make room for you.'

'No, I quite see that,' said Daphne, putting on a brave face, though she felt a little miserable. She had *so* hoped that June would think that she was too brilliant to leave out.

'Cheer up!' said June, giving the girl a little pat. 'There's always next term, and if you go on at this rate, you're an absolute certainty for the team then. In fact, I shouldn't be surprised if you didn't turn out to be the star player!'

This *did* cheer up Daffy enormously, though the girl

might not have felt quite so happy if she had known what Violet had in store for her.

Violet, accompanied by Faith, had been into town to collect the photographs of the first-form picnic, and the two girls now sat side by side on a sofa in the common-room, poring over them. They were alone, for the others were at lacrosse practice, or horse-riding, or walking in the fresh air. Neither Violet nor Faith, however, cared for fresh air, especially when it was cold, and much preferred being indoors, huddled up by the fire.

'This one that Katie took of the two of us is awfully good,' said Faith. 'Do you think that I might have a copy to send home to my people?'

'Of course,' said Violet. 'I say, Faith, this is a nice one of the whole form. Except for me, of course, for I was taking the photograph.'

It was a very nice photograph, the first formers sitting in a row in the sand, their happy smiles showing what a marvellous time they were having. And Daffy Hope was right in the centre of it. At once, Violet decided that Felicity simply had to see that photograph – though how she was going to achieve that was something she hadn't thought out yet.

The girl threw a sidelong glance at Faith, whose head was still bent over the photograph. She hadn't meant to say anything to her about her plan to get Daffy into hot water, but suddenly it occurred to her that two heads might be better than one. Besides, the temptation to boast was becoming too hard for Violet to resist.

She put her head close to Faith's, and said in a confiding tone, 'Shall I tell you a secret?'

Faith nodded eagerly, and Violet went on, 'I mean to make sure that this photograph falls into Felicity Rivers's hands.'

'Why?' asked Faith, puzzled.

'Don't you remember?' said Violet. 'Felicity told Daffy that she wasn't to take part in our picnic, but Daffy disobeyed her. And if Felicity sees this photograph she will know it, and come down hard on Daffy.'

Violet sat back and waited for Faith to congratulate her on this clever plan. But she was disappointed, for Faith was quite horrified.

'Violet, you simply can't do such a thing!' exclaimed Faith. 'Why, sneaking is just about the lowest thing that you can do, and if any of the others were to find out, they would never forgive you.'

Violet frowned at this, and said rather sullenly, 'Well, I think Daffy deserves it. She has been horrible to me, and shown no respect at all towards you, as head-girl.'

Faith couldn't deny this, and said, 'I agree that Daffy needs a lesson, but I'm not sure that this is the way to go about it. Look here, Violet, let's think about it for a bit. Wait until after half-term, and if you are still determined to go ahead with your plan then, I will back you up.'

Violet wasn't entirely happy with this, but she agreed, saying, 'I suppose I can afford to wait another week. In the meantime, I shall have to think of a way of getting that photograph to Felicity, without her knowing that it is me who is behind it.'

Violet knew Felicity's views on sneaks only too well, for she had overheard the Head Girl scolding a second former only a few days ago. Hilda, the second former, had gone to Felicity to report that another member of her form had played a mean trick on her, and Felicity had said rather scornfully, 'Really, Hilda, if you are going to come running to me, or to Miss Parker, every time someone plays a childish trick on you, I'm afraid that you are going to make yourself very unpopular with the rest of your form. Sneaks are considered the lowest of the low at Malory Towers – and at every other decent school, for that matter.'

Seeing that Hilda had turned rather red, Felicity had said in a kinder tone, 'You know that if anyone is deliberately setting out to make you unhappy you can tell me, and I will step in. But tricks like the one you have told me about are just part and parcel of school life, and you must learn to grow a thicker skin.'

No, Felicity would certainly not look favourably on Violet if she simply went and handed her the photograph. She would have to think of a much more cunning way of doing it.

In the meantime, though, there was half-term to look forward to, and the whole school, from the youngest member of the first form to the oldest member of the sixth, got caught up in the excitement.

The beginning of the week seemed to go very slowly,

then there were only three days left, then two, and suddenly it was the day before half-term.

Mistresses and top formers became used to the sight of the younger girls skipping along the corridors, laughing and chattering noisily, but they were lenient with them, for they knew that the girls were just giddy with excitement at the thought of seeing their people again.

The sixth formers, of course, behaved with more restraint, but inwardly they were just as thrilled as the youngsters. Several of them found it hard to get to sleep on the night before half-term, but none of them was tempted to talk or whisper after lights out, for such things simply weren't done when one was in the top form.

It was otherwise in the first-form dormitory, where the girls made so much noise that it brought Matron in on them.

'My goodness, what a dreadful racket there is in here!' cried Matron, snapping on the light and making the first formers blink. 'Off to sleep at once, all of you, or you'll be fit for nothing tomorrow.'

'But, Matron, we're so excited it's simply impossible to sleep!' protested Katie. 'Can't we talk for just ten more minutes?'

'Not even ten more seconds!' said Matron sternly. 'If I hear another sound from this dormitory, I shall personally telephone each and every one of your parents in the morning and tell them that half-term is cancelled!'

Of course, the first formers knew that Matron had no intention of carrying out her threat, but not one of them, not even Daffy, dared to flout her orders. And after she left, there wasn't a sound from the dormitory, as the girls fell asleep, one by one.

They were woken by the sound of the dressing-bell, and in every dormitory in the school the cry went up, 'Wake up, everybody! It's half-term!'

A super half-term

Felicity was delighted that her parents were among the first to arrive, for it meant that she was able to spend a little time alone with them.

'I hope you don't mind, Mother and Daddy,' she said, 'but I have asked someone to join us for lunch. Her name is Alice, and her parents aren't able to come today.'

'Poor girl,' said Mrs Rivers, her ready sympathy stirred. 'Of course we don't mind. Daddy and I thought that we would take you to a restaurant today, as it's a little cold and windy for a picnic.'

Felicity was quite happy about this, and she felt thrilled when Miss Grayling made a point of coming over to speak to her parents, saying, 'Felicity is doing a simply marvellous job as Head Girl. Not that I ever doubted she would, of course.'

'We are very proud of her indeed,' said Mr Rivers, his face glowing with pride.

'And rightly so,' said Miss Grayling with a smile. 'Of course, she has also been working very hard at studying for her exams – as have most of the sixth formers. I hope that all of the girls will put them out of their minds this weekend, and concentrate on enjoying themselves instead.'

The sixth formers were determined to do just that, and Felicity saw many of her friends as she looked around.

There was Bonnie, with her doting parents, and Amy with hers. Lucy strolled arm in arm with her pretty mother, and June shared a joke with one of her brothers. It really was a very happy scene indeed.

The first formers were also having a grand time, though there had been bad news for Faith. Her parents had telephoned Miss Grayling at the last moment to say that they would not be able to come because one of Faith's young brothers was ill. The others had been very sympathetic, for it was very hard to have to stand and watch on a day like this, while everyone went off with parents, grandparents, brothers and sisters to have a jolly time. Daffy felt very sorry for Faith, and decided that she would ask her parents if Faith might come along with them, but Violet spoke up first, laying a hand on Faith's shoulder, and saying, 'Never mind, old girl! You can come along with my people and we will be very pleased to have you.'

This was said in an extremely loud voice, so that the whole of the form would overhear and think what a kind, generous person Violet was. In fact, the only person who was fooled was Faith herself, who was very grateful indeed and thanked Violet profusely.

The others rolled their eyes, Katie muttering to Ivy, 'Her Highness just wants to make Faith feel grateful to her, for then she will have an even greater hold on her.'

'Yes,' agreed Ivy. 'And it will provide Violet with a

marvellous opportunity to boast to Faith, and show off, and prove what adoring parents she has.'

Violet's parents might have been adoring, but they quite failed to impress the first formers.

The girls giggled when they set eyes on Mr Forsyth, who was short and round, and it was quite clear to see where Violet had inherited her turned-up nose and small eyes from. He also seemed rather short-tempered, his expression habitually irritable, except when he was talking to his darling Violet.

'Gosh, I'm glad *my* father isn't like that,' whispered Daffy to Katie. 'And Violet's mother is simply awful!'

This was rather unfair, because Mrs Forsyth wasn't really awful at all, just a rather weak and silly woman, always pandering to the whims of her overbearing husband and spoilt daughter.

Violet squealed when she saw her parents' big, expensive car pull up in the drive, glancing round quickly to make sure that the others were watching before she ran to greet her people.

'My little princess!' cried Mr Forsyth, his discontented look replaced by a fat smile, as he held his arms out to Violet. She ran into them at once, enveloped in a big hug, before turning to Mrs Forsyth, who bent to kiss her cheek.

'We've brought someone else to see you, as well,' said Mr Forsyth with a laugh. 'Here you are, Princess!'

He reached into the back seat of the car, emerging a few moments later with the most beautiful cat the first formers had ever seen. She was very sleek and aristocratic-looking, cream-coloured with chocolate tipped ears and tail, and with brilliant blue eyes.

'She's been pining for you,' Mr Forsyth was saying. 'So I thought to myself, why shouldn't Willow join in the fun of half-term and come to see her mistress.'

Violet was absolutely delighted to see her pet, of course, taking the cat from her father and crying, 'Willow! Oh, how marvellous! Look, everyone!'

The first formers crowded round, for most of them were very fond of animals and were keen to take a closer look at Willow. Violet was very gratified indeed at their exclamations.

'How lovely she is!'

'What marvellous eyes!'

'May I stroke her, Violet?'

'Fancy bringing a cat to visit at half-term. I say, Violet, you're going to have to be awfully careful that she doesn't leap out of your arms while you're carrying her around. She might run off and get lost.'

'Oh, I shan't need to carry her,' said Violet with rather a smug smile. 'Daddy, did you bring the lead?'

'Of course, Princess,' said Mr Forsyth, reaching back into the car to bring out a lead, which exactly matched the cat's blue velvet collar.

'You can't put a cat on a lead!' cried Daffy. 'I never heard of such a thing!'

'Just watch,' said Violet, thoroughly enjoying being the centre of attention. Deftly she clipped the lead on to

121

Willow's collar, then set the cat down on the ground. She walked a few yards, and the girls were both amused and astonished to see that Willow padded along beside her as obediently as any dog.

'Well, I never!' said Ivy. 'How super!'

Daffy, who was not at all pleased at the attention Violet was getting, suddenly grinned and nudged Katie, whispering, 'Watch out for fireworks! Here comes Potty. I'll bet that *she* won't think it's at all *super* to have a cat wandering round and getting under everyone's feet at half-term!'

Indeed, Miss Potts looked a little disapproving when she first spotted Willow, nor did she care for Mr Forsyth, who, on seeing her frown, said rather pompously, 'Ah, you're Violet's form mistress, aren't you? Now, Violet told me your name – I shall remember it in a second. Ah yes, Miss Potty! Look here, Miss Potty, my wife was none too keen on me bringing Violet's pet along, for she thought that there might be some objection. But as you can see for yourself, Willow is very well-bred and well-behaved, and so she should be, for I paid a pretty penny for her, I can tell you!'

Miss Potts's frown deepened, as Violet turned red and the rest of the first form giggled.

'My name is Miss Potts,' said the mistress rather pointedly, adding stiffly, 'And as for the cat, I really don't think . . .'

But her words tailed off, for Willow decided that she rather liked this tall, stern-looking woman, and rubbed herself against Miss Potts's ankles, purring loudly. Miss Potts, who was secretly quite fond of cats, bent to stroke the pretty little creature, and, somewhat to her own surprise, found herself saying, 'Well, as long as she is kept on a lead, I am sure that it will be all right, just this once.'

Then, as though to make up for this moment of weakness, she snapped, 'Katie! Your parents have just arrived, and as they have come a long way, I suggest that you go and greet them, instead of standing there with an idiotic grin on your face.'

The Rivers were nearby when Daffy Hope's people arrived, the two sets of parents greeting one another happily, for they were old friends.

'Well, Felicity!' said Mrs Hope, once she had hugged an excited Daffy. 'It seems like only yesterday that you were starting out as a first former at Malory Towers, and now here you are, Head Girl!'

'And speaking of first formers, how is young Daffy settling in?' asked Mr Hope, a big, good-humoured man. 'I'll bet she's as good as gold, just like her older sister was.'

Felicity looked at Mr and Mrs Hope, their faces shining with pride in their younger daughter. Then Daffy caught her eye, a pleading expression on her face, and Felicity's lips twitched. She certainly didn't want to upset the Hopes, today of all days. Besides, it really wasn't her place to report Daffy's bad behaviour to them. That was up to Miss Potts, or Miss Grayling herself. So Felicity said, 'I think I can safely say that Daffy is going to leave her mark on Malory Towers,' and received a grateful smile from the younger girl.

Mr and Mrs Hope seemed satisfied with her reply too and, as she watched the family walk away, Felicity found herself hoping that Daffy would not let them down.

All of the girls spent a very happy morning with their parents, proudly showing them round the school, introducing them to their friends and talking to mistresses. Then it was time for lunch, and everyone went off with their people to different restaurants.

Violet's parents, of course, had chosen a very expensive restaurant, and Faith, who had never been to such a place before, was quite overawed as she followed the family inside. The girl felt very nervous of Mr Forsyth, and his loud, rather pompous manner, though fortunately he took little notice of Faith, devoting himself to Violet instead.

Mrs Forsyth, however, rather liked the quiet, shy girl, and thought how pleasant it was to be with someone so softly spoken and undemanding for a change. So the two of them enjoyed a nice chat over lunch, and Faith soon lost her nerves and began to think that Violet's mother was really rather sweet.

Willow, of course, was unable to come into the restaurant, and had been left in her basket in the car, and Faith didn't know whether to be shocked or amused when Mr Forsyth ordered an extra portion of chicken and instructed the waitress to wrap it up, so that the cat might share in the treat!

The restaurant that Felicity's parents had chosen was

less expensive, but very nice indeed, and Alice thanked Mr and Mrs Rivers for inviting her along.

'That's quite all right, my dear,' said Mrs Rivers with a smile. 'I am just sorry that your own parents couldn't come.'

She thought that Alice was rather a strange girl, so nervous and eager to please, but she seemed pleasant enough, and Mrs Rivers was glad that Felicity had taken her under her wing.

They enjoyed a most delicious lunch, and it was as they were having pudding that Mr Rivers said, 'Well, exams next week for you two girls. I expect that you will be glad when they are behind you and you can relax a bit.'

'I certainly will,' said Felicity with feeling. 'Alice isn't going in for Higher Cert though, lucky thing!'

'No, I'm not clever enough,' said Alice with her nervous little laugh. 'And even if I was, I'm not very good at settling down to study. I lose concentration too easily.'

Mr Rivers looked surprised at this, and said, 'Well, I don't know anything about how good your brains are, but I should have thought that after all your years at Malory Towers you would have learned how to knuckle down and study.'

'Yes, but Alice hasn't *been* at Malory Towers for years, dear,' said Mrs Rivers. 'Remember, Felicity told us that she only joined the school at the beginning of this term.'

'But I've seen you before, I'm certain of it,' said Mr Rivers, staring hard at Alice from beneath his dark eyebrows. 'Are you quite sure that you only started this term?'

Felicity looked up sharply, glancing first at her father, then at Alice, who had turned bright red, and was blinking rapidly behind her glasses.

Seeing that she was quite tongue-tied, Mrs Rivers came to the rescue, saying, 'Really, Alice ought to know when she started at Malory Towers.'

'I think I must have one of those commonplace faces,' said Alice at last, finding her tongue. 'Several of the girls say that I look familiar to them, isn't that so, Felicity?'

Felicity nodded, but her mind was working rapidly. So her father recognised Alice, too! The whole thing just got more and more peculiar!

Felicity got the opportunity to have a word alone with her parents before they left to go to the hotel they were staying at, and she said, 'I just wanted to thank you both for such a marvellous treat, and for letting Alice share in it, for it has been the most marvellous day! And there's still tomorrow as well, before we have to get back to the grindstone.'

Mrs Rivers was about to say something when her husband suddenly clicked his fingers, and exclaimed, 'Got it!'

'Got what?' asked Felicity and Mrs Rivers, completely puzzled.

'Now it's gone!' said Mr Rivers, looking most annoyed. Then he saw that his wife and daughter were watching him in bewilderment, and gave a laugh.

'Just for a moment, I had a sudden flash of memory,' he said. 'Something to do with Alice, but then it vanished before I could grasp it.'

'Oh, Daddy!' cried Felicity. 'Well, if it comes back to you, do let me know. Quite a few of us girls feel that there is something familiar about her, and we are sure that she is keeping some secret from us.'

'Well, when someone is guarding a secret, it is often because they are ashamed of something,' said Mrs Rivers, sounding very wise. 'But secrets usually come out, sooner or later. And when Alice's is revealed, I hope that you and your friends will be kind, Felicity, and not judge her harshly.'

'Of course not,' said Felicity. 'I just wish that I could get Alice to confide in me, for it would be far better if she told someone the truth rather than it just coming out.'

'Well, perhaps between us we can try to coax her out of her shell a little tomorrow,' said Mrs Rivers.

But the following morning, after breakfast, Alice came up to Felicity, and said, 'I'm awfully sorry, but I don't think that I will be able to come out with you and your people today. I feel rather sick, so I'm going to go and see Matron.'

'What a shame!' said Felicity. 'Well, if you feel better later, do come and join us.'

But, as Alice went off to find Matron, Felicity couldn't help wondering if she was just making an excuse, for the girl didn't look ill, and her appetite had seemed good at breakfast.

'Blow!' thought Felicity. 'I think Daddy scared her a little yesterday, and now it means that Mother and I won't have the chance to talk to her today. Oh well, at least it will be nice to have my parents to myself!'

Violet's parents came over again on Sunday, and, once again, they brought Willow with them, the little cat attracting lots of attention from the girls as Violet paraded her around on her lead.

Even the sixth formers and the parents were amused, Nora saying to her mother, 'My goodness, just look at that! I wonder what our old moggy at home would do if I tried to walk him on a lead.'

'I should think that he would run away and we would never see him again,' laughed Nora's mother.

Two people who weren't amused, however, were Mam'zelle Rougier and Mam'zelle Dupont, and both of them united in their belief that Malory Towers was no place for cats.

'It is bad enough that we have that creature in the stable,' said Mam'zelle Dupont, shaking her head. 'The one that tried to attack me. Now we must have cats at half-term too!'

'What next?' said Mam'zelle Rougier, her thin, stern face set in lines of disapproval. 'Are we to allow pet dogs, and rabbits and mice at Malory Towers?'

Mam'zelle Dupont gave a faint shriek at this, for the thought of mice always filled her with terror, and she and Mam'zelle Rougier linked arms and went indoors, where no cats lurked to disturb their peace.

Faith was very taken with Willow, and rather envious of Violet for being mistress of such a beautiful pet.

'How I wish that she could stay at Malory Towers with us,' the girl sighed as she stroked and petted the cat. 'My word, wouldn't it make the others sit up and take notice!'

'Yes,' said Violet, staring hard at her friend. 'Yes, it jolly well would! Faith, what a marvellous idea. I shall keep Willow here at school with me.'

'But, Violet, you can't!' cried Faith, quite aghast. 'I was only joking, you know. Why, Miss Grayling would never allow it!'

'Ah, but I'm not going to ask Miss Grayling,' said Violet, a smile spreading over her face. 'I shall smuggle Willow into school, and we shall keep her there in secret. None of the mistresses will know that she is there.'

The first formers would be simply thrilled, thought Violet, and wouldn't that be one in the eye for Daffy Hope! Even she did not have enough daring to smuggle a pet into the school.

Once again Faith tried to protest, but it was too late. Violet was running across the lawn to her parents, who were sitting on one of the benches, and putting her idea to them.

Faith, leading Willow, followed more slowly, and reached the bench in time to hear Mrs Forsyth say, 'Violet, you can't! Why, you would be expelled if any of the mistresses discovered Willow. Think of the disgrace! Besides, Willow is a very valuable cat, what if she runs away?'

But Mr Forsyth brushed his wife's protestations aside, saying testily, 'Nonsense! Now, my dear, you know very well that you and I were thinking of going on a little holiday shortly. I am quite sure that Willow would be much happier here with her mistress while we are away, than at home with only the gardener and housekeeper for company. And I'm sure that my princess is quite clever enough to keep her away from the prying eyes of the teachers.'

'Of course I am,' said Violet happily, knowing that her father would overrule her mother, and she would get her way. 'There is a little box-room just above our dormitory, where no one ever goes, and Willow will be quite safe in there.'

'But that won't be good for her!' said Mrs Forsyth. 'She needs to be taken out every day and given exercise.'

'She will be,' said Violet. 'I shall put her inside my coat and take her out every day, when there's no one around. And if I'm not able to do it, there will be no shortage of willing helpers.'

'Oh, dear!' wailed Mrs Forsyth. 'Faith, what do you think of this idea?'

Faith hesitated. She badly wanted to back up Mrs Forsyth, but Violet was her friend, and she would have to endure days of sulks and tantrums if she went against the girl. So Faith swallowed, and said, 'I'm sure that, between us, we first formers can make sure that Willow is looked after, and that no one discovers her. It would be such fun to have her at school.'

'That settles it then,' said Mr Forsyth, clapping his hands together. 'Willow stays at Malory Towers!'

Shocks and surprises

The girls were all pleasantly worn out after their busy half-term, but the first formers were reluctant to go to bed, each and every one of them determined to stay up until the bell went. They were in the common-room when Violet and Faith, having just said goodbye to Mr and Mrs Forsyth, came in, carrying a large wicker hamper between them.

'Oho, what's this?' said Ivy, sitting up straight. 'Goodies?'

'Not exactly,' said Violet as she and Faith set the hamper down on the floor. 'It is something very nice though.'

'Well, don't keep us in suspense,' said Daffy. 'Let's have a look.'

Violet lifted the lid of the hamper and reached in. There were gasps of amazement as she lifted out Willow, and Jenny said, 'Violet, have you gone quite mad? You can't possibly have Willow here at school with you! Miss Potts will soon discover her, then she will be sent home.'

'Oh no, she won't,' said Violet coolly. 'I intend to keep Willow in the little box-room upstairs.'

Then she looked round at the first formers, and said with a smile, 'I hope that some of you will help me to feed her, and take her for walks.'

Of course, almost everyone wanted to help look after Willow, apart from one girl – and that was Daffy.

'It's cruel,' she said. 'Willow is used to roaming around in your big house. You can't possibly keep her cooped up in a box-room.'

'You didn't think it was cruel when you put Queenie into Mam'zelle Dupont's handbag,' said Violet. 'In fact, you thought that it was rather a good joke.'

For once, the ready-witted Daffy was lost for words, and could only glare at Violet.

'Let's take her up to the box-room now,' said Maggie. 'We shall have time to settle her in before bedtime.'

'We had better not all go,' said Faith. 'If Matron or Miss Potts comes along and see us all trooping upstairs they will smell a rat.'

'That's true,' said Violet. 'You and I must go, of course, Faith. Then Maggie and Ivy, you follow in a few minutes, but make sure the coast is clear first.'

The four girls had great fun making Willow feel at home, fussing her and petting her.

'She has had plenty to eat today,' said Violet. 'And she had a walk just before we brought her in, so she should be fine overnight.'

'If we turn the hamper on to its side, and put this old blanket in there, it will do for a bed,' said Faith. 'It's probably not what Willow is used to at home, but it will do.'

'Yes, and someone had better go to the shop tomorrow and buy her some food,' said Ivy, tickling the cat under the chin. 'She can't be fed on scraps all the time, for that won't be good for her.'

The four returned to the common-room just before the bell for bed-time went, and Violet was besieged by a crowd of eager girls, all offering to help look after her pet.

'I can help to feed her, Violet!'

'Oh, do let me take her for a walk! I'll be very careful that no one sees us.'

'I would so love to play with her, for she will need company at times.'

'There will be plenty for everyone to do,' said Violet, casting a sly glance at Daffy, who hadn't said a word.

The girl had been thinking hard, though. Everyone wanted to be Violet's friend now. But it wasn't because they liked her, it was simply because they wanted to share in the fun of looking after the cat. And, knowing Violet, thought Daffy, it wouldn't be very long before the novelty of being popular went to her head, and she began queening it over everyone. When that happened, her brief spell of popularity would soon be over.

Daffy also realised that if she stood out against the others, and refused to take an interest in Willow, it would look like sour grapes on her part.

So she returned Violet's sly look with a sweet smile, saying, 'Count me in, too, Violet. I have always wanted a cat of my own, and helping to look after Willow will be the next best thing.'

Violet looked rather surprised at this, but as the bell went for bed-time then, she said nothing.

As she snuggled down in bed, though, her thoughts were pleasant ones. Everyone wanted to be friends with her now, and soon she would win the whole form over. Why, even that horrid Daffy Hope had asked if she could help care for Willow. Violet smiled to herself in the darkness as she thought of Daffy, for the girl had a shock coming to her. Somehow, Violet was going to make sure that Felicity found out that the girl had been at the picnic, then Daffy would really be in hot water!

'I simply must think of a way for Felicity to see that photograph, without her knowing that it is me who is behind it,' said Violet to Faith, the next morning.

'But, Violet, you can't possibly go ahead with your plan now!' said Faith.

'I don't see why not,' said Violet, frowning. 'You agreed with me that Daffy needs to be taught a lesson.'

'Yes, but don't you see?' said Faith. 'You are not in a position to stir up trouble for *anyone* now. If you sneak on Daffy, and she so much as suspects that you are behind it, she will retaliate by letting it slip that you have smuggled Willow into the school. Then you will be in as much trouble as she is – probably more!'

Violet bit her lip, for this had not occurred to her.

'Blow! Yes, I suppose that you are right, Faith. Well, I shall just have to think of some other way of getting back at Daffy.'

As it happened, though, Felicity *did* find out about Daffy's disobedience, and it was Faith – quite unwittingly – who was responsible.

Violet and Faith had been putting the photographs of the picnic into an album one Saturday afternoon, and, as they finished, Violet said, 'Faith, would you be a dear and put the album on my cabinet in the dorm? I must go up to the box-room and feed Willow, for she will be starving.'

As Violet ran up the back stairs leading to the little box-room, Faith made her way to the dormitory, but as she turned a corner, she walked smack into a third former, and the album flew from her grasp.

'Hey, watch where you're going!' said the third former, glaring at Faith before going on her way.

'Well!' thought Faith. 'Of all the nerve! It was as much her fault as mine.'

The girl quickly picked up the album, but – in her haste – didn't notice that one of the photographs had fallen out. And Felicity, walking down the same corridor a few minutes later, found it.

She picked it up, smiling at the happy faces that grinned up at her. Why, it was a photograph of the first-form picnic! Then, quite suddenly, Felicity's smile vanished, replaced by a grim expression. For there, in the centre of the photo, looking as if she was having a marvellous time, was Daffy Hope!

So, Daffy had disobeyed her, and gone to the picnic after all! Well, she would be punished for it, that much was certain.

Susan was in her study as Felicity walked by, a stern look on her face, and she called out to her friend.

'Whatever has happened?' she asked. 'You've got a face like thunder!'

Felicity dropped the photograph on Susan's desk, saying, 'Just take a look at that!'

Susan studied the photograph, then looked up at Felicity, a puzzled frown on her face.

'It's the kids at their picnic,' she said. 'But I don't see what there is in that to put you in a temper.'

'Look again,' said Felicity. 'And you will see that there is someone there who shouldn't be.'

Susan did look again, and gave a gasp. 'Daffy! The sly, deceitful little beast! I must say, she is as different from her sister Sally as can be!'

'Yes, Sally is absolutely straight and honest,' said Felicity. 'And Daffy isn't. It's one thing to be naughty and mischievous, but outright deceit and disobedience is something I will not tolerate.'

'I should jolly well think not!' said Susan indignantly. 'What a shame that you should have to deal with it now, though, right in the middle of exams.'

'Well, I'm not going to deal with it now,' said Felicity. 'I shall send for Daffy, and tell her that I know what she has done, but I won't punish her until after the exams are over. Then I shall have leisure to come up with a really fitting punishment!'

'And Daffy will have a week or so in which to ponder her fate, and think about what is going to happen to her,' said Susan, with a grim smile. 'That is quite a punishment in itself.'

'Well, it's no more than she deserves!' said Felicity crossly, going across to the door.

'Hi, Eileen!' she called out, to a passing second former. 'Run along to the first-form class-room, would you, and tell Daffy Hope to come to my study at once.'

'Yes, Felicity,' said the second former obediently, and ran off.

Daffy was surprised, but not alarmed, when Felicity's message was delivered, for it did not occur to her for a second that she could be in trouble. It didn't do to keep the Head Girl waiting, so Daffy obeyed the summons at once.

She was rather surprised by Felicity's stern expression, then she remembered that the sixth formers were taking Higher Cert at the moment, and all of them were feeling the strain.

'Hallo, Felicity,' she said brightly. 'Eileen said that you wanted me.'

'I do,' said Felicity, getting straight to the point. 'Daffy, it has come to my notice that you attended the first-form picnic, after I expressly forbade you to do so. What do you have to say?'

For a moment, Daffy was unable to say anything at all, for she was quite lost for words!

The girl could only stare at Felicity in horror as she wondered how on earth the Head Girl had found her out.

At last, she said, 'Yes, I did go to the picnic, Felicity. I'm sorry that I disobeyed you.'

'Are you?' said Felicity. 'Or are you sorry that you have been caught out?'

'Both,' said Daffy truthfully. She had enjoyed every moment of the picnic, but now that she was about to get some perfectly horrid punishment, she wondered if it had been worth it!

Daffy felt very uncomfortable as Felicity stared hard at her, and wished that the Head Girl would just get it over with and reveal what her punishment was to be.

She was quite astonished, therefore, when Felicity said, 'Very well, you may go now.'

'But – but aren't you going to punish me?' stammered Daffy.

'Oh, yes,' said Felicity coolly. 'But not today. Please come and see me at the same time next Saturday, when I shall have decided what to do with you.'

Daffy's heart sank. She might have known that she wouldn't get off that lightly! The girl walked towards the door, then a thought occurred to her, and she turned, saying, 'Felicity! How did you find out that I had disobeyed you?'

'That is none of your business, Daffy,' said Felicity. 'But I hope it will be a lesson to you that lies and deceit are usually found out eventually.'

Daffy was thoughtful as she made her way back to the common-room. Who had known that she had been ordered not to go on the picnic? Katie, of course, but Katie was her best friend and would never sneak on her. Who else could it be? Of course! Faith had known, for she had spoken to Daffy about it just before the picnic, and been most disapproving. The girl had sworn that she wouldn't sneak, but she must have, for how else could Felicity have found out?

Everyone but Violet was in the common-room when Daffy entered, a scowl on her face as she slammed the door behind her.

'What's up?' asked Katie, looking alarmed. 'Don't say that Felicity gave you a scold.'

'It's worse than that,' said Daffy, flinging herself down into an armchair. 'I'm to be punished, because someone has split on me.'

At once the first formers crowded round Daffy.

'Split on you? Why, what have you done?'

'Did Felicity find out about that trick you were going to play on Mr Young?'

'Don't say that someone told her you sneaked into the second form's dormitory the other night!'

'No,' said Daffy. 'She found out that I disobeyed her by going to the picnic, after she had forbidden me to.'

A gasp went up for, of course, most of the first formers didn't know that Daffy had been banned from joining the picnic.

'Well, I have to admire your nerve,' said Ivy, after the whole story had been told. 'No wonder Felicity was furious!'

'But who could have split on you?' said Katie, who had been puzzling over this. 'I was the only person who was in on the secret, and you surely can't think it was me!'

'I know that it wasn't you, Katie,' said Daffy. 'But

someone else did know, and that person must have told Felicity.'

The first formers followed the direction of Daffy's hard stare, and they realised that she was looking at Faith.

'Faith, is this true?' said Jenny, looking shocked. 'Did you sneak to Felicity?'

'Of course she did,' said Daffy scornfully. 'Faith didn't approve of me disobeying our Head Girl at all, did you, Faith?'

'No, I didn't,' answered Faith, stung by Daffy's unjust accusation. 'As a matter of fact, I don't approve of a lot of things that you do, Daffy. But that doesn't mean that I would sneak on you.'

Into this tense atmosphere walked Violet, and she realised at once that something was wrong.

'Did you know that your friend was a cowardly little sneak, Violet?' asked Katie.

'What on earth are you talking about?' asked Violet, quite astonished.

'Faith knew that Felicity had said I wasn't to go on the first-form picnic,' said Daffy. 'And Felicity has found out that I disobeyed her, so Faith must have split on me.'

Violet listened to this with mixed feelings. She was delighted that Daffy was in trouble with Felicity. But she felt sorry for Faith, and as she knew that her friend had strong feelings about sneaks, she felt quite certain that she wasn't the culprit.

Of course, she, Violet, had also known about Felicity's punishment, but she couldn't very well say so, or the others might suspect her of being the sneak!

But, to her credit, she spoke up for Faith, saying scornfully, 'What nonsense! As if Faith would think of doing such a thing!'

'Well, you would stick up for her,' said Jenny. 'The two of you have been as thick as thieves lately.'

'I vote we send her to Coventry!' shouted Katie.

Some of the others murmured agreement, and poor Faith looked ready to faint.

'I shall do nothing of the sort,' said Violet, going across to Faith and taking her arm.

'Then you will be sent to Coventry, too,' said Daffy, in a hard voice.

'That isn't for you to decide, Daffy Hope!' said Violet. 'The others will decide whether they want to send Faith and me to Coventry. But anyone who does won't be allowed to help look after Willow, or play with her.'

This, however, was a mistake. The first formers didn't care for Violet's ultimatum, much as they loved Willow. And Daffy was still unofficial leader of the first form, and a very strong character. So when Katie cried, 'Very well, let's have a show of hands! All those in favour of sending Faith – *and Violet* – to Coventry, please put your hands up now,' every hand went up.

'Well,' said Daffy with satisfaction. 'That's that. Come on, girls, who's for a game of something before tea?'

Daffy is punished

At last exams were over, and the relief among the sixth formers was almost tangible.

'I feel like doing something completely mad!' said June at breakfast one morning. 'Like diving fully clothed from the topmost diving board, or running down the corridor yelling at the top of my voice.'

'Go on, then!' said Freddie promptly. 'I dare you!'

A few years ago, June would have taken Freddie up on this instantly. Now, though, she gave a regretful sigh, and said, 'If only I could! But Miss Grayling would probably expel me for setting a bad example to the kids.'

'Talking of kids,' said Susan to Felicity in a low voice, 'have you decided how you are going to punish Daffy Hope yet?'

'No,' said Felicity. 'I've scarcely had time to think about it. But she is coming to see me this afternoon, so I had better put my thinking cap on.'

'There seems to be some sort of rift within the first form,' said Susan. 'Just look at them now.'

Felicity glanced over at the first-form table, and noticed that Faith and Violet seemed to be seated a little apart from the others. And, although Violet kept up a determinedly bright flow of conversation, Faith looked the picture of misery. What on earth was going on there? Felicity wondered.

She found out later on that day, when she spotted Faith walking down the corridor near the sixth-form studies, a defeated slump to her shoulders and a rather woebegone expression on her face.

Feeling sorry for the girl, Felicity went up to her and said, 'Is everything all right, Faith, old girl?'

The kindness in Felicity's tone and the concerned expression on her face were too much for Faith and, quite suddenly, tears started to her eyes. Seeing them, Felicity quickly laid a hand on the girl's shoulder, guiding her into her study.

There, she shut the door and sat Faith down, saying, 'Well, now, whatever is all this about?'

Faith began sobbing in earnest, and it was a while before she could speak, but at last she dried her tears, and said, 'Oh, Felicity, Daffy and the others have sent Violet and me to Coventry, and it is so unjust of them!'

At the mention of Daffy's name, Felicity's lips tightened, and she said, 'Why have they sent you to Coventry, Faith?'

Faith hesitated for a moment, then she looked at Felicity's warm, open expression, and blurted out, 'Well, actually, Felicity, it's because of you.'

'Me?' said Felicity, astonished. 'You will have to explain more clearly, Faith, for I don't have the slightest idea what you are talking about.'

'Well, someone sneaked to you about Daffy going on the first-form picnic,' said Faith. 'And Daffy has decided that it was me. Of course, Violet stuck up for me, because she is my friend, so the first formers aren't speaking to either of us.'

A sudden thought struck Faith, and she went on, 'Oh, Felicity, if you were to tell Daffy that it wasn't me who sneaked, she and the others would believe you and they would start talking to Violet and me again.'

Felicity was silent as she contemplated all sorts of dire punishments for Daffy. Really, the girl's behaviour went from bad to worse! Not content with being naughty and disobedient, she had made a false accusation against Faith, causing great unhappiness for the girl.

The expression on Felicity's face was so stern that, for a moment, Faith feared that she had said something wrong.

Then the girl smiled, and said, 'Don't worry, Faith. I will be seeing Daffy later, and I will have a great deal to say to her. One thing you may be sure of, though, is that your spell in Coventry will end today.'

Felicity sounded so determined that Faith felt quite reassured, and went off to find Violet in a much happier frame of mind.

Daffy, meanwhile, had decided that her best hope of getting off lightly was to act contritely in front of Felicity, and perhaps even squeeze out a few tears. Only the hardest-hearted people could bring themselves to be unkind to Daffy when she cried, and no one could accuse Felicity of being hard-hearted.

The girl rubbed hard at her eyes as she walked to Felicity's study that afternoon, so that they would look red, and the Head Girl would think that Daffy had been sobbing her heart out as she waited in terror to hear what her punishment would be.

Alas for Daffy, Felicity was not taken in at all!

She steadfastly ignored Daffy's red eyes, and her occasional doleful sniffs, and proceeded to give the girl a scolding which almost reduced her to genuine tears!

'I am very disappointed in you, Daffy,' said Felicity. 'Because you have such a lot of good in you, and could become a worthwhile person, if only you wanted to be. But it seems to me that all you want to do at Malory Towers is play around and make trouble for others with your spiteful ways.'

Daffy reeled at this, for although it was certainly true that she enjoyed playing around, she didn't consider herself a spiteful person at all. Felicity was quite wrong! Just look at how popular she was with the others, and spiteful people were never popular.

'That's not fair, Felicity!' she cried, hurt. 'I'm not spiteful, truly I'm not!'

'No?' said Felicity. 'You have been very spiteful to poor Faith, and to Violet.'

Daffy turned red. How on earth did Felicity know about that?

'Faith has been sent to Coventry because she is a sneak,' said Daffy rather stiffly. 'And Violet stuck up for her, so we are not speaking to her either.'

'Faith is NOT a sneak!' said Felicity firmly. 'And if you are going to set out to judge people, Daffy, it would be a very good idea if you checked the facts first.'

Felicity sounded so very sure that, for the first time a doubt began to creep into Daffy's mind, her heart sinking as she wondered if she had made a very big mistake!

'I didn't find out about your deceit from Faith,' went on Felicity. 'This is what tripped you up, Daffy.'

And Felicity pulled open the drawer of her desk, getting out the incriminating photograph, which she placed in front of Daffy.

The first former gasped, and said, 'Where did you get this from?'

'I found it in the corridor, not far from your common-room,' said Felicity. 'Someone must have dropped it. So, now you see, Daffy, no one sneaked on you. Not Faith, and not any of the others.'

Daffy was horrified. She had accused Faith wrongly, and had encouraged the others to send her – and Violet – to Coventry.

'It was very wrong of me,' she said, sounding most subdued. And, for once, Daffy was not merely pretending to be contrite, she really meant it. And Felicity could tell from the girl's manner that she was sincere. She didn't need to tell Daffy that she owed the two girls an apology either, for the first former went on, 'I shall tell them both that I am sorry, of course, and I shall do it in front of the others.'

'I am very glad to hear it,' said Felicity. 'You know,

Daffy, you seem to have spent rather a lot of time this term apologising to people. If only you would learn from your mistakes, you might not have to say sorry quite so often!'

Daffy nodded solemnly, and Felicity said, 'Now we come to your punishments. Since you avoided the last one, I'm sure you will agree that it is only fair that you receive two.'

Daffy groaned inwardly, but did not protest, for she knew that Felicity was being quite fair and just.

'You are to go to bed one hour early next Saturday night,' said Felicity. 'I know that the first and second formers have been given permission by Miss Grayling to hold a dance in the hall, but I am afraid that you will miss it. And this time, Daffy, I shall be checking personally to make sure that you have obeyed me.'

This was a bitter blow, for the whole form had been looking forward to the dance, but Daffy swallowed hard and said meekly, 'Yes, Felicity.'

'In addition,' Felicity went on, 'as you are so fond of sending people to Coventry, you will send yourself to Coventry for one day. This punishment will also take place on Saturday, and you are not to talk to anyone from the second you get up on Saturday morning until Sunday morning. Nor must any of the others talk to you, and I shall be asking Faith to report to me if anyone breaks the rules. Is that quite clear?'

'Quite clear,' said Daffy faintly. This punishment was even worse than the first, for Daffy loved to chatter, and it would be very difficult for her to keep quiet for a whole day! But she had well and truly earned her punishment, and this time she was determined to face it.

It was with a heavy heart that the girl went back to the first-form common-room. Most of the others were there, and Daffy didn't shirk what she had to do, but went over to Violet and Faith, saying in a clear voice, 'I owe you both an apology.'

The others immediately stopped their chatter, and came round to listen.

'I have just been to see Felicity,' said Daffy, 'and I know now that it wasn't Faith who sneaked on me. I should have made sure before I accused you, and I'm very sorry. Please will you forgive me?'

Faith was a good-natured girl, and she took the hand that Daffy held out to her at once, saying, 'Of course. I'm just glad that it is all over now.'

'Well, we should never have sent you to Coventry, or you either, Violet, and I am sorry about that, too,' said Daffy.

Violet was less gracious, refusing to take Daffy's hand, and merely inclining her head rather coldly.

Some of the others, who had been quick to follow Daffy's lead and only too ready to believe her accusations, murmured apologies too. The outspoken Ivy said roundly, 'You idiot, Daffy! You made us all believe that Faith was a sneak, and we have been quite beastly to her because of it, and to Violet.'

Daffy turned red, and said, 'Well, you may be sure

that I will think twice before I accuse anyone of anything ever again.'

'I'm very glad to hear it,' said Violet with a disdainful sniff.

'You will be pleased to hear that I am being punished,' said Daffy, looking directly at Violet. 'None of you are to speak to me at all next Saturday, and I am not allowed to go to the dance.'

Some of Daffy's friends cried out at this, feeling that it was a very harsh punishment, but Ivy said, 'Well, it jolly well serves you right! And this time, Daffy, I hope that you won't try to get out of your punishment.'

'I won't,' said Daffy ruefully. 'That is another lesson I have learned.'

'If Faith wasn't the sneak, how did Felicity find out that you had been at the picnic?' asked Katie curiously.

'She found one of the photographs,' said Daffy. 'Someone must have dropped it.'

'Heavens, that must have been me!' gasped Faith. 'Violet and I were putting them in an album the other week, and I dropped it when I was taking it up to the dorm. One must have fallen out. So it was my fault that you got into trouble with Felicity after all!'

'Yes, but you didn't get me into trouble deliberately,' said Daffy, patting the girl on the shoulder. 'And that makes a huge difference!'

Felicity, meanwhile, was in her study, telling Susan all that had happened.

'I think that you handled it very well,' said Susan.

'I really do. The thing is, with people like Daffy, you have to come down hard on them or they just take advantage of you.'

'Don't I know it!' said Felicity. 'I say, Susan, what about a walk in the grounds before tea? I could do with some fresh air.'

Susan agreed at once, and as the two girls walked to the door, her sharp eyes suddenly spotted something lying on the floor.

'Here, what's this?' she said, stooping to pick it up. 'Why, it's a silver locket. Rather a nice one, too.'

Felicity took the locket from Susan and inspected it, saying, 'The chain has snapped. I wonder if it belongs to Daffy? She could have dropped it when she was in here earlier.'

'No, for there are some initials engraved on the back,' Susan pointed out. 'And they aren't Daffy's. It says JJ. I don't think I know anyone with those initials, do you?'

Felicity thought hard for a moment, and said, 'There's a girl in the fourth form called Julia Jenks, but she certainly hasn't been in my study, so I don't know how she could have dropped it here.'

'How odd!' said Susan. Then a thought occurred to her, and she said, 'I say, Felicity, you don't suppose that this could have been stolen from Julia, do you? Perhaps the thief dropped it.'

'It's a possibility, I suppose,' said Felicity. 'Though rather a horrible one. And, for all her faults, I don't think that Daffy is a thief.'

'Well, who else has been in your study today?' asked Susan.

'June and Freddie popped in this morning,' said Felicity. 'So did Delia. Oh, and Alice came in to give me back a book that she had borrowed.'

'Well, we can certainly rule out June, Freddie and Delia,' said Susan. 'Though it's true that we don't know much about Alice.'

The two girls looked at one another rather uneasily for a moment, then Felicity said firmly, 'I've just been telling young Daffy off for jumping to conclusions and accusing people wrongly, so I don't intend to fall into the same trap myself. I think that the best thing to do would be to hand it in to Matron, then she can put a notice up.'

As luck would have it, the two girls bumped into Julia Jenks on their way to Matron's room, and Felicity said, 'Julia, have you lost a locket just lately? We have found one with your initials on it.'

Felicity took the locket from her pocket, and Julia said, 'No, it's not mine, Felicity. I only wish it was, for I don't own anything half as pretty as that.'

'Well, what a mystery!' said Susan, as she and Felicity went on their way. 'There is no other girl in the school with the initials JJ, so who on earth can it belong to?'

Getting to know Alice

Felicity soon put the mystery of the locket to the back of her mind, as she had plenty of other things to think about.

Now that exams were over, Amy and Bonnie were spending a lot more time together. But Felicity knew that Alice was still a frequent visitor in Amy's study, and that Amy hadn't invited her there simply for the pleasure of her company.

She sent for Amy one day, and wasted no time in getting to the point.

'You are taking advantage of Alice,' she said bluntly. 'I know that she does all the little jobs that you want to get out of, and it simply isn't fair.'

Amy turned red, and said rather haughtily, 'If Alice chooses to do my jobs for me, I don't see what business it is of yours, Felicity.'

'It's my business because I am Head Girl,' Felicity told her. 'And it seems to me that it is all very one-sided, for Alice isn't getting anything in return.'

'She has my company,' said Amy with a shrug. 'And that is what she really wants, you know – company and friendship. Besides, I don't see any of you others rushing to make friends with her.'

'That's not fair, Amy,' said Felicity. 'You know very well that we have all been busy studying. And now that the exams are over, all that is going to change. I want every sixth former to make an effort with Alice, and try to bring her out of her shell. That includes you, Amy. But I *don't* want to see you using her as a slave, however willing she is, and I would be grateful if you would respect my wishes.'

Rather sullenly, Amy agreed, and when she had left, Felicity went to Alice's study and tapped on the door.

'Come in!' called out Alice, in her high, rather nervous voice. 'Oh, hallo, Felicity. Do sit down.'

Felicity sat, noticing as she did so that Alice had a small photograph album on the desk in front of her. The girl hastily shut it, and Felicity said, 'Are those photographs of your people? May I have a look?'

But Alice quickly slid the album into a drawer, saying hastily, 'It's empty. I bought it the other day, because Mother said that she was going to send me some photographs from home. I'm still waiting for them to arrive, though.'

Felicity knew that this was untrue, for she had seen quite clearly that there were photographs in the album, just before Alice shut it. But if the girl wished to keep them private, Felicity could hardly insist on seeing them.

So she changed the subject, saying, 'You never talk much about your home, or your people, Alice.'

'Well, there's not much to say,' said Alice, blinking

rapidly behind her glasses. 'My parents are quite ordinary, and so is my home.'

Yet Amy was convinced that Alice came from a wealthy family, because of her expensive clothes. Well, perhaps she didn't want to boast about it, thought Felicity, and that was very much to her credit.

'Do you have any brothers or sisters?' she asked.

'Oh no,' said Alice. 'It's just my parents and me. You have a sister, though, don't you? I've heard the others talk about her, and she sounds marvellous.'

So it went on. Each time Felicity tried to draw Alice out, the girl responded with the briefest of answers, before asking a question of her own. So when Felicity left Alice's study a little while later, she knew no more about the girl than she had before. She was standing in the corridor puzzling over this, when a small voice behind her said, 'What are you doing standing there, Felicity?'

Felicity turned, to see that Bonnie had come up behind her, and she was struck by a sudden brainwave.

'Bonnie!' she said, taking the girl's arm. 'Do come into my study for a moment. I want to ask you a favour.'

'What is it, Felicity?' asked Bonnie, sitting down in an armchair.

Felicity looked at little Bonnie for a moment. The girl was very small and dainty, with a childish, lisping voice. In many ways she appeared more like a first former than a sixth former. But Bonnie was very shrewd indeed, and extremely good at sizing people up. She also had a knack of getting people to open up and confide in her, and Felicity had decided that she might come in very useful now.

'Bonnie, I would like you to have a chat with Alice,' she said. 'See if you can get her to talk about herself a bit.'

'Find out what her secret is, you mean,' said Bonnie, with a smile. 'All right, I'll do my best. It won't be easy, for as soon as anyone tries to get her to talk about herself, she clams up, or changes the subject.'

'Some of us feel that she is familiar, as if we have met her before,' said Felicity.

'Yes, I heard some of the others talking about it,' said Bonnie. 'Though I am quite certain that I don't know her. Nor does Amy, and Freddie is sure that she has never met her before. Lucy, Gillian and Delia don't recognise her either.'

Felicity frowned over this, then said slowly, 'You, Freddie and Amy joined Malory Towers in the third form, didn't you? And Lucy came when we were in the fourth.'

'That's right,' said Bonnie. 'And Gillian and Delia didn't join us until the fifth form. What are you getting at, Felicity?'

'Well, as none of you seem to recognise Alice, perhaps she was someone we knew when we were in the first or second form.'

'I suppose that makes sense,' said Bonnie. 'Well, Felicity, leave it to me and I'll see if I can get anything out of her.'

While the sixth formers puzzled over Alice, Daffy was

not having an easy time of it in the first form. Some of the others had been very annoyed with her for falsely accusing Faith of sneaking, and, when her day of being sent to Coventry arrived, found it all too easy to ignore her.

Violet's popularity, on the other hand, had gone up, for the girls were missing Willow and all of them begged to be allowed to help care for her again. Violet had been a little stiff with them at first, but, at last, knowing that it would annoy Daffy, she had graciously forgiven them.

Daffy deeply resented seeing Ivy, or Jenny, or one of the others sneaking off to the box-room with Violet, and it was even harder to bear because she only had herself to blame.

Only Katie remained steadfast and loyal, but Daffy knew that she would have to work hard to win back favour with the others.

Inspiration came to her when she received a letter from her grandmother one breakfast-time, and she opened it to find that it contained a substantial postal order.

She slipped it into her pocket without saying anything to the others, but an idea had taken root in her mind, and she thought about it all day.

That evening, in the common-room, she stood up and clapped her hands together loudly, to get everyone's attention.

'Listen!' she cried. 'It seems to me that it has been a little dull around here lately, and I think that it's time we livened things up.'

'What are you going to do?' called out Violet. 'Start a

big row by flinging wild accusations around?'

Daffy swallowed the retort that sprang to her lips, put on a contrite expression, and said, 'Actually, I was hoping to make amends to you all for that.' She pulled the envelope from her pocket and waved it in the air, saying, 'My grandmother sent me a postal order today, with instructions to spend it on anything I please. And what would please me more than anything would be to throw a midnight feast for you all!'

Of course, this caused a perfect hubbub, the eyes of the first formers lighting up. Even Violet couldn't help looking pleased at the prospect of a feast.

'My word, that's awfully generous of you, Daffy!'

'I should say. A feast – what fun!'

'Of course, we others will contribute something as well.'

'When shall we have it?'

'What about next Wednesday evening?' suggested Katie. 'Potty is away that evening, for I overheard her telling Matron so.'

'Next Wednesday evening it is, then,' said Daffy, beaming round. 'We can have it in the dormitory, and use that big cupboard on the landing to store our goodies in.'

There were 'oohs' and aaahs' at this, and Ivy said, 'Jenny, shall you and I pop into town before tea tomorrow, and buy some biscuits or something?'

'I shall buy another of those big chocolate cakes, like the one I got for our picnic,' said Violet. 'I say, wouldn't it be super if Willow could come, too?'

Many of the girls thought that this was a splendid idea, but Daffy said, 'Of course Willow can't come! You would have to trail all the way up to the box-room to fetch her, and then go and put her back again once the feast was over. And the more we wander about, the more chance there is of us being caught.'

The others reluctantly agreed with this, and Daffy muttered under her breath to Katie, 'I don't want that pampered little beast at my party.'

'Which pampered little beast are you talking about?' asked Katie, her eyes alight with mischief. 'Violet or Willow?'

Daffy laughed at this, her spirits lifting as she looked round at the happy, excited faces of the others. The thought of a feast had brightened everyone up, and put her back in their good books. And Daffy intended to see that she stayed there!

Bonnie, true to her word, asked Alice to go into town with her the next afternoon.

'Amy is busy, and I do so hate going on my own,' said Bonnie. 'I really would like your company, Alice, and you can help me carry my shopping.'

Of course, the idea of helping Bonnie appealed to Alice enormously, and she agreed at once.

Now that exams were over, Bonnie was happy to have leisure to pursue her favourite hobby of needlework and, as they reached the little town, she said to Alice, 'I can set to work making that cushion cover I promised you now. Let's go into the haberdashery shop, and you can choose the fabric and embroidery silks.'

'Oh, Bonnie, that would be marvellous!' cried Alice, thrilled. 'Of course, I shall pay for all the materials. But are you sure you wouldn't prefer to make something for yourself?'

'No, for there is nothing I need at the moment,' said Bonnie. 'I am just happy to have something to work on. Besides, I promised you a cushion cover, and that is what you shall have.'

The two girls spent a pleasant half hour in the haberdashers, and Bonnie was surprised to find that, for someone so diffident and timid, Alice had very definite ideas on what she wanted. Although, in Bonnie's opinion, her taste wasn't very good.

The girl chose a deep, purple fabric, and a variety of brightly coloured silks for the embroidery. When Bonnie ventured to suggest that perhaps fewer colours might look more effective, Alice brushed this aside, saying, 'I like colourful things. And my father sends me as much money as I wish, so I can afford to buy a few extra skeins of silk.'

Unseen by Alice, Bonnie raised her eyebrows at this, for it was the first time that the girl had referred to her family's wealth. Though she had said it quite matter-of-factly, and not in a boastful way, as Amy, or that conceited little first former Violet, might.

'Well, that was fun!' said Bonnie, as the two of them left the little shop, Alice carrying her purchases in a large brown paper bag.

'Yes, it was,' said Alice, smiling. 'I say, Bonnie, there's

a little tea-shop across the road. Let's go in and have a cup of tea and some cake – my treat, as a thank you for being kind enough to make me one of your lovely cushion covers.'

Bonnie accepted gratefully, and soon the two girls were comfortably seated at a little table by the window, chatting happily together as they tucked into delicious jammy buns, washed down with big cups of tea.

A harassed-looking woman with twin daughters, aged about eight, came in and sat at a table near theirs, the two little girls talking at the tops of their voices as they vied for their mother's attention.

'Heavens, what a din!' said Bonnie, grimacing. 'I must say, I'm awfully glad that I'm an only child, for I should hate to have to share my parents' affection, wouldn't you, Alice?'

Alice, who found Bonnie's company very pleasant and relaxing, considered this for a moment, her head on one side. 'I used to feel like that,' she said at last. 'But now I think that it might have made me a better person if I had had a brother or sister.'

Bonnie was careful not to show any surprise at this remark, for she knew that Alice would clam up. Instead, she laughed, and said jokingly, 'I'd rather be a spoilt brat than a good person.'

'But you are a good person, Bonnie,' said Alice earnestly. 'I know that your parents adore you, for I saw you with them at half-term. But I'll bet they don't give you everything you ask for.'

'No, for they can't afford to,' said Bonnie honestly. 'They aren't fabulously wealthy, as Amy's parents are. They give me their love unstintingly, though. Sometimes too much.'

'*Can* you give someone too much love?' asked Alice, surprised.

'Sometimes you can give them too much of the wrong kind of love,' said Bonnie. 'You see, Alice, when I was small I was quite ill, and had to be taken great care of. And, even when I got better, Mother would insist on wrapping me up in cotton wool.'

'Oh!' said Alice, who had had no idea of this. 'Well, I suppose it is understandable, for she must have been very worried about you.'

'Of course,' said Bonnie. 'And I quite see that now. But when I was younger, I often found it quite annoying and wanted to rebel against it and stand on my own two feet. And yet, I always find it comforting to know that my parents are there, ready to help me if I am in trouble, or comfort me if I am sad, just as they were when I was a small child.'

Alice was very struck by this, and said, 'Yes, that is how I feel about my mother and father.' Then she went quiet, and Bonnie, sensing that she was building up to something, said nothing, but nibbled at her cake and appeared quite unconcerned. At last her patience was rewarded, and Alice blurted out, 'I wish that I didn't feel ashamed of them, but Father does embarrass me so, at times!'

'Really?' said Bonnie, sounding as nonchalant as possible. 'How?'

But Alice seemed to realise that she had said too much, and retreated right back into her shell. All Bonnie could get from her after that was polite chit-chat. But the girl was not dismayed, for Alice had given away a lot more than she knew.

Pam, Nora, June, Freddie and Susan were in Felicity's study that evening when Bonnie went to report to her. Quickly, she told them what had happened and, in disgust, Nora said, 'Well, what a waste of time, Bonnie! As far as I can see, all that you did was went shopping and had tea and cakes! Very nice for you, but it doesn't really get us any further!'

'My dear Nora,' said Bonnie, shaking her head. 'It is precisely because of that attitude that Felicity chose *me* to talk to Alice, and not *you*!'

Nora looked rather put out, while June, who had a great deal of respect for Bonnie, laughed, and said, 'Come along, Bonnie! Tell us what you *really* learned about Alice.'

'Very well,' said Bonnie. 'I learned that she has been spoilt, and used to having her own way, but that she has tried hard to change. I learned that she loves her parents, but is ashamed of them. And, perhaps more importantly than anything else, I learned that she is ashamed of herself – or, at any rate, of something that she did in the past, which she would now like to make amends for.'

Freddie gaped at Bonnie, open-mouthed, and

said, 'How on earth can you know all that?'

'Bonnie listens to people,' said Felicity, getting up and giving the girl a pat on the shoulder. 'And there is no one quite as good as her at reading between the lines. Well done, Bonnie.'

'Yes, I take my hat off to you,' said Pam. 'I don't think that any of us others would have been quite as successful as you at getting Alice to open up.'

'I agree,' said Susan. 'But, despite Bonnie's efforts, we are really no further forward, for we still don't know why Alice is so familiar to us. Well, to most of us, anyway.'

'Yes, we are,' said June, a very thoughtful look on her face. 'It's as if we have a jigsaw, and must put the pieces together. Bonnie has given us a few of the pieces, but there are still some missing. All we have to do is find them.'

Several of the first formers had been into town that day, too, to buy food for their midnight feast.

The big cupboard outside the first-form dormitory gradually filled up with goodies over the next few days, and as Daffy and Katie opened it one morning, to put in a tin of biscuits that Ivy had just given them, their eyes lit up.

'Scrumptious!' sighed Katie happily. 'Tinned sardines and pineapple, chocolate, gingerbread cake – ooh, and an enormous pork pie! How marvellous!'

'It's going to be the best feast ever,' said Daffy, placing the tin of biscuits on a shelf.

And it would clinch her place as leader of the first form,

thought the girl, though she did not say this to Katie.

As the day of the feast dawned, the first formers grew increasingly excitable and giggly, almost driving Miss Potts and Mam'zelle Dupont to distraction.

'Really, I don't know what is the matter with this class today,' said Miss Potts in Maths on Wednesday morning. 'I have already had to tell Maggie off for daydreaming, and Ivy for chattering. And it is quite obvious to me that none of you have your minds on your work. Well, if you don't knuckle down and give me your full attention, I'm afraid that you will have to make up for it by doing an hour's extra prep tonight.'

Of course, none of the first formers wanted that, so they decided that they had better settle down and behave.

Mam'zelle, who took the first form for the last lesson of the day, grew very vexed at their restlessness and threatened all kinds of dire punishments. Even the quiet Faith chattered animatedly to Violet, bringing the French mistress's wrath upon her head.

'Ah, even you, Faith, who are normally so good and so obedient – even you plague me today. I shall send you to bed one – no, two – hours early tonight. I shall send the whole *class* to bed two hours early!'

As the whole form was simply dying for bedtime to come, this amused them greatly, and Faith thought that Mam'zelle was going to explode with anger when they all started giggling.

Fortunately, Daffy saved the situation, by keeping a

straight face and saying piously, 'Come, now, girls, you are all taking advantage of Mam'zelle's good nature, and it won't do!'

Then she smiled sweetly at the French mistress, and said, 'The thing is, Mam'zelle, we are going on a lovely, long nature walk tomorrow afternoon, and we are all looking forward to it so much that I am afraid everyone has become a little over-excited.'

Mam'zelle accepted this explanation readily, for she knew how these English girls adored their country walks, even when the weather was bad. Though it seemed very odd indeed to her! But Daffy's contrition, coupled with her pretty smile, soothed her a little, and she said more calmly, 'Well, you will all please forget about your walk for the moment, and concentrate on your French. Anyone who displeases me will miss the walk, and come to me tomorrow afternoon for extra coaching instead!'

Violet, who did not care to be outside in the cold weather, didn't know which was worse – a nature walk, or extra French coaching! But as the others had no intention of missing out on their walk and settled down, the girl decided that she had better do the same.

Shortly before tea that day, Miss Potts came up to Felicity, and said, 'I am sorry to ask you this at such short notice, Felicity, but I wonder if you would mind looking in on the first formers before you go to bed tonight? I am going to the theatre with a friend, you see, and shall be staying the night with her. Miss Parker had agreed to look in on them for me, but she has been taken ill with flu and is in bed.'

'Yes, of course I will do it, Miss Potts,' said Felicity at once. 'You can rely on me.'

Jenny of the first form, who happened to be walking by, overheard this, and dashed off to tell the others the news.

'Jolly good!' said Ivy. 'I daresay Felicity will want to get off to bed, so she will probably just pop her head in at the door on her way up and not trouble us again.'

'Yes, and she's a jolly good sport anyway,' said Maggie. 'I bet that even if she did catch us having a feast she wouldn't split.'

Daffy, who knew only too well just how stern Felicity could be on occasion, wasn't so certain of this. But, as the Head Girl would be safely tucked up in bed by the time the feast began, she wasn't terribly worried about it.

There was a great deal of laughing and chattering after lights out that evening in the first-form dormitory. Daffy, of course, was in the thick of it, and Faith, who had just about given up trying to control the unruly first formers, lay silently in her bed and said nothing. But, as time went on, she nerved herself to raise her voice, saying, 'I say! Hadn't we better settle down before Felicity does her rounds?'

Many of the others ignored this, and carried on talking, but when Daffy backed Faith up and said, 'Faith is quite right. Besides, we had better get some sleep or we shall never be able to wake at midnight,' there was immediate silence.

Faith did not mind this at all, but Violet felt resentful on her behalf, and, in the darkness, her lips tightened. She made no comment, though, for the girl had something else up her sleeve, and, when the feast began, Daffy would soon see who was the most popular girl in the first form.

At last, one by one, the first formers dropped off to sleep, and when Felicity gently pushed open the door, shortly before eleven o'clock, there wasn't a sound to be heard. Felicity smiled to herself as she pulled the door softly to behind her. The first formers were such little monkeys this term that she had half-expected to be called upon to break up a pillow fight, or some such thing. Thank heavens that they were all fast asleep, for she was longing for her own bed.

An hour after Felicity had looked in, the little alarm clock that Daffy had placed under her pillow went off, startling her into wakefulness. For a moment she couldn't think why the clock had gone off when it was still pitch dark, then she remembered, and sat up excitedly in bed, hugging her knees and smiling to herself. It was time for the midnight feast – *her* midnight feast!

Midnight feast

Quickly, Daffy padded round the dormitory, waking all the sleeping girls. Silently, they climbed out of bed, putting on dressing-gowns and slippers.

'Katie and I will fetch the things from the cupboard,' whispered Daffy. 'Ivy, there are some plates under my bed that I managed to borrow from the kitchen. Jenny and Maggie, you fetch tooth mugs, so that we have something to drink out of. Faith, you and Violet . . . I say, where *is* Violet?'

'She can't have gone far,' said Faith. 'For she was here a minute ago. Perhaps she has gone to the bathroom.'

But Violet hadn't gone to the bathroom. The girl was quite determined that Willow would be at the feast, and she was tiptoeing upstairs to the box-room to fetch her pet.

The little cat was very pleased to see her mistress, for she was feeling rather bored and restless, and she mewed as Violet stooped to pick her up. It sounded very loud in the still of the night, and Violet whispered, 'Shush now, Willow, or you will get me into the most awful trouble. Come along, let's go and join the feast.'

Then Violet tucked the cat into the front of her

dressing-gown and made her way back to the dormitory.

The others were busy setting all the food out on plates in the middle of the floor when she returned, and everyone looked up in alarm as the door opened.

'Oh, it's you, Violet!' said Katie. 'My goodness, what a start you gave me. Where have you been?'

'Never mind that,' said Daffy crossly. 'For heaven's sake, shut the door behind you, quickly, Violet. And someone had better put a couple of pillows along the bottom, where the gap is, then we can put the light on.'

Ivy quickly pulled the pillows from her own bed, arranging them along the bottom of the door, before switching on the light. Then she gave a gasp, as she saw Willow's head poking out from Violet's dressing-gown.

'Willow!' she cried. 'Oh, Violet, you brought her after all. How marvellous!'

'For goodness sake, keep your voice down!' hissed Daffy, before turning to Violet and saying angrily, 'I told you that you weren't to bring Willow to the feast.'

'Why should I do what you say?' said Violet, tossing her golden curls. 'You aren't head of the form, though you sometimes behave as if you are.'

'No, but it's my feast,' said Daffy. 'And I have the right to say who comes and who doesn't. I've a good mind not to let you share in it, Violet!'

Violet was about to make a sharp retort when Jenny said, 'We can hardly throw Violet out of her own dormitory while we enjoy the feast. Besides, she has provided us with that lovely tin of sweets, as well as that delicious-looking chocolate cake, so it wouldn't be fair not to let her share.'

'Very well,' said Daffy with bad grace. 'But that cat had better not cause any trouble.'

'She will be as good as gold,' said Violet, removing Willow, who was beginning to wriggle, from her dressing-gown and placing her on the bed.

Then the first formers sat on the floor, in a big circle, and settled down to enjoy their feast.

'Scrumptious!' sighed Maggie, taking a bite of pork pie. 'Simply scrumptious.'

'You know, I normally hate sardines,' said Ivy. 'But for some reason I can eat no end of them at a midnight feast.'

'Well, save some for the rest of us!' laughed Ivy. 'I say, Faith, pass the ginger beer, would you?'

The girls ate hungrily, until all that was left was the chocolate cake, sweets and biscuits.

'Shall I cut the cake?' asked Violet.

'Yes, do,' said Jenny. 'I feel awfully full, but I daresay I shall find room for a slice.'

But it was as Violet finished cutting the cake that Willow, who had behaved very well throughout the feast, sitting on the bed, being fed the occasional tit-bit and watching the proceedings with interest, decided to take a little exercise.

The cat suddenly leapt from the bed, landing right in the middle of the cake and showering Daffy, who had just leaned forward to take a slice, with crumbs, chocolate and cream.

There was a horrified silence, and everyone waited for Violet to throw a tantrum and scold the cat. But, to everyone's astonishment, she threw back her head and laughed until the tears poured down her cheeks. One by one, the others started to laugh too, for Daffy really did look comical with cream all over her face and crumbs everywhere.

Daffy, however, was not at all amused. That beastly cat had ruined her feast, and made her a laughing stock! Had it been one of the other girls who had been covered in cake, Daffy would have joined in the laughter with everyone else, but although the girl liked to play jokes, she didn't care to be on the receiving end of them, and felt extremely humiliated.

'It's all very well for you to laugh,' she hissed. 'But just look at the state of my dressing-gown! I shall get into a dreadful row with Matron, and it's all your fault, Violet, for bringing that cat in here.'

'I'm sure that we can get the worst of it out, without Matron knowing anything about it,' said Katie soothingly, seeing that Daffy's feathers were seriously ruffled. 'Come on, let's go along to the bathroom and see what we can do.'

The two girls went out quietly, the muffled laughter of the others ringing in Daffy's ears and making her feel simply furious.

'That horrid cat!' she said to Katie, once the two of

them were in the bathroom. 'I wouldn't be a bit surprised if Violet had trained her to do that, just as I was leaning over.'

'I don't think that one *can* train cats,' said Katie doubtfully, thinking of her own cat at home. 'They seem to do pretty well as they please.'

'Well, it's all her fault, anyway,' said Daffy. 'I ordered her not to bring it to the feast and she went against my wishes. I'll pay her back for this, somehow, Katie, you see if I don't!'

'What are you going to do?' asked Katie, her eyes wide.

'I don't quite know,' answered Daffy. 'But I'll think of something, you may be sure.'

Then the two girls set to work sponging Daffy's dirty dressing-gown. Fortunately, it was as Katie had said, and they managed to get most of the sticky mess that the cake had made off it. Then Daffy washed her face and rinsed her hair, thinking that she should be sitting with the others, enjoying the biscuits and sweets, instead of wasting time like this – and at her own feast, too!

The others had cleared away the ruined cake when Daffy and Katie returned to the dormitory, and Violet, glancing at Daffy's wet hair, couldn't resist saying, 'My word, Daffy, you do look a drip.'

The others laughed at this, and it was just too much for Daffy, who gave the girl a shove. It wasn't a particularly hard or violent shove, but the unexpectedness of it caught Violet off balance, and she fell against one of the bedside cabinets. Unfortunately, two large, heavy bottles of ginger beer were perched precariously there, and they fell to the floor with a resounding crash.

The first formers stood rooted to the spot, gazing at one another in horror and, at last, Maggie whispered, 'Do you think anyone heard that?'

'I should jolly well think they did!' said Faith, beginning to collect the plates up. As head of the form, she would be held responsible if they were caught out. 'Come on, everybody, don't just stand there! There's a very good chance that one of the mistresses will be upon us in a minute.'

That thought made the first formers spring into action, and they scurried round, pushing bottles, empty tins and all other evidence of the feast under beds and into cabinets.

Violet, meanwhile, scooped up Willow, and said, 'I must get her back to the box-room quickly.'

'There isn't time,' said Faith. 'If one of the mistresses comes along and finds your bed empty, you will really be in hot water! You'll just have to take Willow into bed with you, and do your best to keep her quiet.'

'This is all your fault, Violet,' said Daffy with a scowl. 'If you hadn't brought Willow to the feast –'

But Faith, for once, wasn't taking any nonsense from Daffy, and she interrupted to say sternly, 'This is no time to argue over who is to blame. Get into bed at once, Daffy – all of you, in fact – and settle down.'

For a moment it looked as if Daffy was going to argue

with Faith, too, but then the girls heard the unmistakable sound of footsteps approaching, so she quickly scrambled into bed and snuggled down under the covers, closing her eyes tight. The others did the same, Violet putting Willow right down under the bedclothes, and praying that the cat wouldn't give herself away by mewing.

Everyone held their breath as the footsteps got closer, the landing light clicked on and, at last, the door opened. The first formers wondered which mistress had heard them. Stern Mam'zelle Rougier, perhaps? Or the hot-tempered Mam'zelle Dupont? Worse still, what if the noise had roused Miss Grayling herself?

But, as the light from the landing showed, it was none of these feared mistresses who stood in the doorway. It was Felicity!

In fact, the crash the bottles had made hadn't been quite as loud as the girls had feared, and hadn't woken anyone. Felicity, however, had been unable to get to sleep, for, although she was tired, something was playing on her mind. At last she remembered that she hadn't gone back to her study before going to bed, and had left the light on in there. Inwardly groaning with annoyance, the girl had got out of bed and gone to her study, which was directly below the first formers' dormitory. That was when she had heard the crash, and, as Miss Potts was away, had gone to investigate.

All of the girls were in their beds, apparently sound asleep, as she opened the door, and Felicity began to wonder if the noise had come from somewhere else. But, just as she was about to leave, a nervous, smothered giggle came from Maggie's bed. Instantly suspicious, Felicity snapped the light on, and a few of the girls sat up slowly, blinking.

'Felicity!' said Daffy, with a very convincing yawn. 'Is something wrong?'

'I heard a noise from this dormitory,' said Felicity, staring hard at the girl. 'A very loud noise.'

'Well, we didn't hear anything,' said Katie, rubbing her eyes. 'Perhaps you were mistaken, Felicity.'

Felicity's instincts told her that she hadn't been mistaken at all, and that the first formers had been up to something. Then, glancing down, she saw a pile of biscuit crumbs in the middle of the floor, and she knew. The little monkeys had been having a midnight feast! Felicity's lips twitched, as she instantly made up her mind not to report the girls to Miss Potts. It would have been quite another matter if they had broken a very serious rule, such as leaving their own tower, but a feast was just a bit of fun, and something that most schoolgirls' enjoyed at some time. Felicity had certainly enjoyed them when she was lower down the school.

'Perhaps I was mistaken,' said Felicity, her eyes twinkling. 'Faith, you are head of the dormitory, aren't you? Well, perhaps you will see to it that it is thoroughly tidied before Matron does her rounds tomorrow. I am sure that you don't want to get an order mark, for that really would – er – take the biscuit!'

Those girls who were sitting up stared at their Head

Girl in astonishment, while the ones who were pretending to be asleep could hardly believe their ears. Then Felicity went, shutting the door softly behind her. As soon as the sound of her footsteps died away, a flurry of whispering broke out.

'Well, isn't Felicity decent?'

'Golly, what a sport!'

'I always knew that old Felicity was a good sort!'

'I say, Violet, thank heavens Willow didn't mew and give herself away!'

'Yes, she's fallen asleep, thank goodness,' said Violet. 'Perhaps I had better take her back to the box-room now.'

But Faith, taking a stand, said firmly, 'No, we'll have no more wandering around tonight, for we have been jolly lucky so far. Violet, she will have to stay here tonight, and you must take her back in the morning, before we go down to breakfast.'

'All right, Faith,' said Violet, pleased at the thought that she would have her beloved pet with her all night.

Some of the girls began to whisper again, and Faith said, 'We'll have no more talking, either. You never know, Felicity might take it into her head to come back, and I don't think she would be so lenient with us a second time.'

And, much to her surprise and pleasure, the first formers fell silent immediately, and in a very short time, all of them were fast asleep, worn out by their late night.

Everyone found it very difficult to get out of bed the next morning, and again Faith took charge.

'Violet, do get up!' she begged, shaking the girl. 'You must get Willow back to the box-room at once! And you others, we need to sweep these crumbs up and clear all the rubbish from under the beds. There is no time to waste!'

Groaning, the girls reluctantly got out of their warm, cosy beds.

'I feel sick!' groaned Maggie, clutching her stomach. 'I can't possibly eat any breakfast.'

'You must eat a little,' said Katie. 'Or the mistresses will guess that something is up. Though, I must say, I don't feel terribly hungry myself.'

'I don't suppose any of us do,' said Faith. 'Ivy, run along and see if you can find a dustpan and brush, would you? And Jenny, do you mind taking the plates back to the kitchen? The rest of us will clear this rubbish away.'

But one person still remained in bed, the covers over her head, and that was Daffy. Faith frowned, for she didn't see why the girl should get out of the cleaning up. She walked across to Daffy's bed, and said, 'Come on, Daffy, there's work to be done.'

'Just five more minutes,' mumbled Daffy sleepily.

'No, Daffy!' said Faith sharply. 'We need everyone to pitch in if we are to have the dormitory tidy before we go to breakfast.'

Slowly, Daffy sat up and looked round the room, at the first formers all busily tidying up, and she said, 'I don't see dear Her Highness pitching in! It's too bad, especially as she was responsible for spoiling the feast.'

'You know very well that Violet is hiding Willow away,' said Faith. 'And as for her spoiling the feast – well, Daffy, you were the one who pushed her, and that is what caused the bottles to crash to the ground.'

'She had already spoiled it before that,' said Daffy, getting out of bed. 'By allowing that cat of hers to jump on the cake.'

'Oh, I don't know,' said Ivy, returning with the dustpan and brush in time to hear this remark. 'Personally, I thought it was jolly funny.'

'It was,' agreed Maggie with a grin. 'What a pity Violet didn't have her camera ready. She could have taken a marvellous photograph of you, Daffy, all covered in chocolate cake!'

Daffy was most displeased, especially when Ivy handed her the dustpan and brush, saying, 'Make yourself useful, Daffy!'

The girl toyed with the idea of flatly refusing, but she sensed that many of her form were still feeling cool towards her, partly because she hadn't made Willow welcome at the feast, and partly because she had pushed Violet and brought things to an abrupt end. It really was most unfair, thought Daffy. She had suggested the feast so that she could get back into the good books of the first formers, but the opposite had happened – and all thanks to that silly Violet!

All in all, it wasn't a good morning for the first formers. Maggie felt so sick after breakfast that she was sent to Matron, and given a large dose of extremely nasty-tasting medicine. And the whole class was so tired and inattentive that both Mam'zelle Rougier and Miss Potts gave them extra prep as a punishment.

Most of them agreed that it had been worth it though, for they really had enjoyed the feast. And Violet had enjoyed it most of all, for not only had she annoyed Daffy by bringing Willow to the feast, but she had had the pleasure of seeing her enemy humiliated. She really would have to buy Willow a special treat for that!

Daffy, however, was extremely subdued and downcast – until tea-time, when she was struck by a simply marvellous idea for getting back at Violet.

'Katie,' she whispered to her friend. 'Come to one of the little music-rooms after prep tonight. There is something I simply have to tell you.'

So, after prep, the two girls sneaked away to one of the little music-rooms, and Katie, looking at Daffy's mischievously sparkling eyes, said eagerly, 'What is it? You're up to something, I can tell.'

Daffy grinned, and said, 'I have worked out how I am going to teach Her Highness a lesson.'

'How?' asked Katie at once.

'By taking away something that she values,' said Daffy. 'Listen carefully, Katie. This is what we are going to do.'

A shock for Violet

An outbreak of flu ran through the school over the next week, and it seemed that half of the girls and several of the mistresses went down with it.

June was in despair, for several of her best lacrosse players were taken ill, and she groaned to Freddie, 'We shan't have a hope of winning our matches at this rate! Even some of the reserves have gone down with this beastly flu, so I am going to have to make up completely new teams.'

Poor Matron was run off her feet for, as she complained to Miss Potts, 'No sooner do I get one sick girl back on her feet and out of the San, than someone else goes down with it.'

'Well, let's just hope that you don't catch this wretched flu, Matron,' Miss Potts had replied. 'I don't know what we should do without you to care for all these sick girls.'

Violet and Maggie were both confined to the San for several days, and although Maggie was pleased to be under Matron's expert care, Violet fretted terribly about Willow.

'Don't worry,' Faith assured her when she came to visit one day. 'The rest of us are taking great care of her.'

But there was a dreadful shock in store for Violet on the day that she returned to class. Of course, she wanted to satisfy herself that Willow hadn't pined away without her, and before the first lesson started, she and Faith made their way up to the box-room.

'Willow!' Violet called softly, as she pushed open the door. 'Willow, I'm back.'

She waited for the cat to pad across the floor to her, purring loudly, but Willow did not appear.

'How odd!' said Faith. 'She usually comes running as soon as someone opens the door.'

Violet looked rather worried, then she heard a purring sound coming from the cat's basket, and she walked across and peered in. Then she gave a little shriek, which startled Faith and made her rush to Violet's side, saying, 'Violet, do be quiet! No one must know that we are here.'

'Yes, but look, Faith!' said Violet, lowering her voice a little. 'Willow is gone, and this – this *creature* – is in her place.'

Faith looked down at the basket – and gasped. For there, instead of the sleek, well-fed Willow, was Queenie, the stable cat!

As though sensing Violet's disapproval, Queenie suddenly leapt out of the basket and fled through the open door. She knew where she wasn't wanted!

'I thought you said that Willow was fine,' said the distressed Violet, rounding on Faith. 'You told me that you and the others were caring for her.'

'We were,' said Faith, feeling quite shaken. 'Why, I fed her myself just before breakfast. And Ivy took her out on the lead immediately afterwards.'

'Ivy must have left the door open then,' said Violet. 'And Willow has got out. Why, she could be anywhere!'

'Of course Ivy didn't leave the door open,' said Faith. 'For it was firmly closed when we got here.'

'Someone has stolen her then,' said Violet, a look of horror crossing her face. 'It's the only explanation.'

'But who would steal her?' asked Faith in astonishment.

'You'd be surprised,' said Violet solemnly. 'She is very valuable, and anyone who knows anything about cats would be able to tell that at once. Someone could have been passing and looked in through the fence when we were exercising her, and made up their mind to take her.'

'Yes, but how on earth would they have got in to the school?' asked Faith, not quite convinced.

'It wouldn't be too difficult,' said Violet. 'Why, there are often strangers here, if you think about it. Only yesterday a man came to mend the piano. And there are always butchers and bakers and so on delivering food to the kitchen.'

'I suppose that's true,' said Faith. 'Or perhaps one of the maids could have discovered her. I don't think that they earn an awful lot of money, you know.'

'I never even thought of that,' said Violet, looking quite horrified. 'Faith, we must get Miss Grayling to telephone the police at once!'

'We can't,' said Faith. 'If you tell Miss Grayling that you have been keeping your pet cat here all these weeks she'll be simply furious. Why, she might even expel you. No, Violet, we must solve this ourselves.'

'Yes, I suppose that we must,' said Violet, close to tears. 'Poor, dear Willow, I do hope that she hasn't come to any harm.'

In fact, Willow was very comfortable indeed. Daffy and Katie – for it was they who had taken her – had found her a home in an old shed behind North Tower that was no longer used. The two girls had lined a cardboard box with a blanket, and had made sure that the cat had plenty of food and water.

'We'll have to exercise her, too,' said Daffy as they watched the cat settle in. 'But we must be jolly careful that no one spots us.'

Katie said nothing, for although she had gone along with Daffy's plan, she didn't feel at all happy about it, and said so.

'I don't like it, Daffy. It's stealing!'

'Of course it's not, silly,' laughed Daffy, brushing this aside. 'We are going to give Willow back to Violet, in a few days, so how can it possibly be stealing? I'm just teaching her a lesson, that's all.'

'Well, I wish you had thought of another way,' said Katie miserably. 'I think it's rather a cruel thing to do, to both Violet and Willow. And I don't see why you had to put Queenie in Willow's place!'

'Oh, that was just for a joke,' said Daffy. 'Dear Violet is

such a little snob I just wanted to picture her expression when she found a common moggy like Queenie in her precious Willow's place.'

But Katie was not in the mood to be amused, saying worriedly, 'I expect that Violet will have discovered Willow is missing by now.'

Katie was not at all reassured when she saw Violet's pale, stricken face in the Maths lesson a short while later. As for Miss Potts, she was so alarmed by the girl's appearance that she wanted to send her straight back to Matron.

'It's quite all right, Miss Potts,' said Violet, struggling to speak normally. 'I would rather be in class.'

Miss Potts, who had dismissed Violet as spoilt and lazy, was encouraged that she was showing some strength of character, and said kindly, 'Very well, but you are not to overdo things. Just sit quietly and read your book, Violet, while I go through some sums on the blackboard with the others.'

'Are you quite sure that you are all right, Violet?' asked Jenny, in the common-room that evening. 'You've been awfully quiet all day.'

Violet exchanged a glance with Faith, who said, 'I think that you should tell the others what has happened. After all, the more people who are looking out for Willow, the more chance you have of finding her.'

So, her voice almost breaking, Violet told the others what had happened to Willow. Of course, there was a perfect outcry.

'Who on earth would do such a mean thing?'

'Don't worry, Violet, old girl. I feel quite certain that no harm will come to Willow.'

'Yes, do try not to worry, Violet, though it must be awfully difficult not to.'

Daffy did not add her voice to the others. She had hoped to let Ivy and one or two others in on the joke, and suddenly realised that they would not think it was funny. For the first time, the enormity of what she had done was beginning to dawn on her, and she was regretting her actions. What was more, she felt a pang of conscience as she looked at Violet's pale, unhappy face, and very uncomfortable it was too!

'Well, the whole of the first form is behind you, Violet,' said Ivy. 'If there is anything we can do to help find Willow, we will do it.'

There were murmurs of agreement from everyone, even Daffy and Katie, who thought that they had better say something, or it would look very suspicious! But both girls felt sick with guilt.

Meanwhile, there had been drama in the sixth form, too. It had happened in Miss Oakes's English class when Alice, who, Felicity noticed, had been looking rather peaky, stood up to go to the mistress's desk. The girl swayed on her feet, gave a moan, and then crumpled to the floor.

'Good heavens!' cried Miss Oakes. 'June, go and fetch Matron at once, please.'

June sped from the room, returning a few moments

later with Matron. Alice had revived a little by this time, and was sitting up, while Miss Oakes bent over the girl, holding her hand.

'Well, now, what have we here?' said Matron in her brisk but kindly way as she bustled in. 'My goodness, Alice, you do look pale.'

She stooped and placed a cool hand on Alice's hot forehead, saying, 'Just as I thought, you've caught a dose of this nasty flu that's going around. A few days' rest in the San, and you will be as right as rain. Miss Oakes, do you think you could help me get Alice to her feet?'

'Of course,' said the mistress, taking one of the girl's arms. Matron took the other and, between them, they helped Alice to stand up, though the girl looked as if she might have collapsed again, if it hadn't been for the support of Matron's strong arm around her waist.

Matron helped Alice from the room, and Felicity said, 'Poor old Alice! She looked awfully white.'

'Well, she is in good hands with Matron,' said Miss Oakes. 'I only hope that none of you others have caught the flu.'

Lucy and Gillian had already gone down with it, but were now back in class, feeling 'as good as new', as Lucy put it. The others, however, had escaped the illness and, over the next few days, didn't let the fear of catching it put them off visiting Alice.

Matron would not allow any visitors on the day that she had been taken ill, but the following afternoon she announced that Alice was feeling a little better and might have two visitors. So, shortly before tea, Susan and Pam went along to the San, and were pleased to see Alice sitting up in bed, with a little more colour in her cheeks. She had been given a little room of her own, just off the main San, Matron explaining, 'I have two second formers and one first former recovering rapidly in the main San, and as Alice needs peace and quiet, I thought that she would be better off in here on her own.'

'Poor old thing!' said Pam, handing the girl a bottle of barley sugar.

'The others all send their love,' said Susan. 'I shall be able to tell them that you are looking a little better.'

'I feel a little better, too,' said Alice with a weak smile. 'Matron has taken such good care of me. It's awfully dull, though, sitting here in bed, with nothing to do.'

'Well, Felicity is coming to see you tomorrow,' said Pam. 'I shall ask her to bring you a book.'

The three girls chatted amiably, until Matron came to shoo Susan and Pam out, saying, 'Alice is going to have some tea now, and then I hope that she will get a good night's sleep.'

Matron escorted them out, and, once they were back in the main San, Susan suddenly remembered something.

'Matron!' she said. 'Did anyone ever claim that locket that Felicity and I handed in to you? The one with the initials JJ on it?'

'Yes, someone did, as a matter of fact,' answered Matron.

'Who was it?' asked Susan curiously. 'Apart from Julia

Jenks, Felicity and I simply couldn't think of anyone with those initials.'

But, before Matron could answer, one of the second formers yelled out and demanded her attention.

'I'm coming, Jane!' called Matron. 'And I'm not deaf! There really is no need to shout *quite* so loudly!' Then she turned back to the sixth formers, shaking her head. 'Honestly, girls, these youngsters are running me ragged. Tell Felicity that she may come and see Alice tomorrow.'

'Blow!' said Susan, as she and Pam stepped out into the corridor. 'I never did find out who the mysterious locket belonged to.'

'Mysterious locket?' said Pam, raising her eyebrows. 'Do tell.'

Susan told the girl all about the locket that she and Felicity had found, and Pam laughed, saying, 'Didn't it occur to you that the locket might have been handed down to one of the girls by her mother or grandmother? The initials on it could have belonged to them, and not to whoever owns it now.'

'Of course!' said Susan, her brow clearing. 'I never thought of that. What a shame, I thought that we had stumbled on a good mystery.'

In the first-form dormitory that evening, Katie took Daffy aside as the girls got ready for bed.

'Daffy, even you must realise that we can't keep Willow away from Violet any longer. We must put her back in the box-room.'

'I know,' said Daffy, looking slightly shamefaced. 'I

only meant it as a joke, to pay Violet back for spoiling the feast, but I realise now that I shouldn't have done it. Don't worry, though, Katie, we will simply sneak Willow back into the room when no one is around. And nobody will ever guess that we had anything to do with it.'

Alas for the two girls, sneaking Willow back into the room proved more difficult than either of them had anticipated. The following morning, they discovered that one of the maids had taken it into her head to sweep the landing just outside the box-room, and they had to retreat hastily down the stairs before Willow, wriggling violently inside Katie's coat, escaped.

'I'm sure that landing hasn't been swept for weeks,' said Daffy crossly as they took the cat back to the shed. 'Why on earth did someone have to decide to clean it today, of all days?'

'Well, we have half an hour free this afternoon,' said Katie. 'We can try again then.'

But once more the girls' plans went awry, as they had to spend their free half hour explaining the disappearance of some new stockings to Matron.

'Perhaps we should slip out tonight, when everyone is asleep,' said Daffy. 'At least we know that no one will be sweeping the landing then, and we will be safe from Matron!'

But Katie had made up her mind that she was going to think twice before becoming involved in any more of her friend's madcap schemes, and she said firmly, 'No! We will just have to wait until tomorrow.'

'No, we won't!' said Daffy suddenly. 'Why, we don't have to get Willow back into the box-room ourselves at all! We will send Violet an anonymous note, telling her that Willow is in the shed. Then she can do it herself.'

'Yes!' cried Katie. 'Why didn't we think of that before?'

That afternoon, while the two first formers composed a carefully worded note to Violet, Felicity was leaving the San, having paid a visit to Alice.

'Thank goodness you have brought me something to keep me occupied,' Alice had said, taking the book that Felicity had brought her. 'I have slept nearly all day, and I'm quite sure that I shall be awake all night.'

'Well, don't let Matron catch you reading late at night,' Felicity had warned with a laugh. 'Or you'll be for the high jump!'

'Felicity!' called out Matron as she saw the girl leave Alice's room. 'Will you take some mending back to Amy for me, please? Why the silly girl persists in darning brown stockings with coloured wool I don't know, for she knows I will only return them to her. Go and wait in my room, while I just give the youngsters their medicine, and I will be with you in a moment.'

Felicity went into Matron's cosy little room, grimacing as she looked at the big bottles of medicine that stood neatly on the shelves. Matron also had lots of photographs pinned up on her walls, of various forms at Malory Towers throughout the years. Felicity smiled as she saw a photograph of her sister, Darrell, and June's cousin,

Alicia, when they had been first formers. And, heavens, there was a photograph of Felicity and her friends when they had been in the second form. How young they all looked! Suddenly, Felicity's glance rested on someone in the front row of the photograph and her smile froze, as she gave a gasp. She took a step forward, to get a closer look, her heart beating fast. It couldn't be – could it? But it was, there was no doubt. Now Felicity knew exactly who Alice was!

A most dramatic night

Daffy and Katie had put the note they had written to Violet in the girl's desk.

'She will find it tomorrow morning,' said Daffy. 'And will rush off to get Willow at lunchtime. Then all our problems will be at an end.'

But Daffy was wrong, for Violet slipped into the empty class-room before tea, to get a book that she needed for prep, and found the note then.

Who on earth could it be from, the girl wondered, ripping open the envelope and pulling out the sheet of paper inside. Her heart pounded, as she read:

Come to the disused shed behind North Tower at 12. Come alone, do not tell ANYONE where you are going, and you will get your cat back.

Violet gave a gasp. Why, it sounded almost like a ransom note – except that whoever had written it had not demanded money.

Of course, Daffy hadn't expected Violet to find the note until tomorrow, and meant her to go to the shed at lunchtime. But Violet thought that she was supposed to be there at midnight tonight!

The thought of going out alone at midnight to meet

the kidnappers was very frightening indeed. Heavens, what if the person who wrote the note was waiting for her? What if she ended up being kidnapped as well? Violet hastily stuffed the note into her pocket, and went to tea, slipping into her seat beside Faith.

She longed to confide in the girl, but it was too dangerous. The kidnappers had said that she wasn't to tell ANYONE.

I know what I shall do! thought Violet. I will write Faith a note and put it on her bedside cabinet, before I go out to meet the kidnappers. Then, if I don't come back, she will read it in the morning and raise the alarm.

Poor Violet felt so scared that she could hardly eat any tea. But, although she was very frightened, the thought of not going never even occurred to her. All that mattered was getting her precious Willow back.

At the sixth-form table, Felicity also had something on her mind, and Susan, who had spoken to her twice without getting a reply, said, 'Felicity, what on earth is the matter with you? You've been in a perfect daze since you went to visit Alice.'

'Sorry,' said Felicity with a rueful smile. 'It's just that I found something out, and I'm rather puzzled about it.'

'Well, are you going to tell me what it is?' asked Susan curiously.

'Yes, but I need to tell the others as well,' said Felicity. She raised her voice, and said, 'Listen, everyone! Please can you all come to my study after prep? There is something that I need to talk to you about.'

Everyone agreed at once, and wondered what it was that Felicity had to say to them. She looked awfully serious!

It was very crowded in Felicity's study that evening as the sixth formers poured in, all of them feeling very curious indeed. Felicity opened the drawer of her desk and pulled out a photograph, which she placed on the desk.

'I borrowed this from Matron,' she said. 'Take a look.'

'My goodness, it's us when we were second formers!' gasped Nora.

'Look, June, there you are in the back row,' said Freddie. 'You've hardly changed a bit.'

But June wasn't looking at herself. She was looking at a plump girl in the front row and, as the truth dawned, her eyes met Felicity's.

'This is all very nice,' said Julie. 'But I don't understand why you have asked us here to look at an old photograph.'

'I do,' said June. 'Take a look at the girl next to Pam, in the front row.'

'I remember her!' said Susan. 'Josephine Jones. What a horrible girl she was. I remember . . . Oh, my goodness! It's her, isn't it? It's Alice!'

'Of course it's not Alice!' scoffed Delia, looking over Susan's shoulder. 'That girl is plump and Alice is thin. And she is fair, while Alice has brown hair.'

'People can lose weight,' said Bonnie, looking at the photo critically. 'And change their hair colour. But they can't change their faces, and that is most definitely Alice's face.'

'There's no doubt about it,' said Gillian. 'Just look at the eyes. It's Alice, all right.'

'Of course, that would explain why she wore glasses with plain glass in them!' said Felicity. 'To try and disguise herself a bit.'

'I don't understand,' said Amy, with a puzzled frown. 'Are you saying that Alice and this Josephine are one and the same? If that is true, why would she try and disguise herself and change her name?'

'Because she knew that we wouldn't want her back here,' said Nora rather scornfully. 'Of course, you girls who joined us higher up the school won't know the story, but Jo was an awful girl – conceited, boastful and thought that she could do as she pleased. She was expelled in the end, after running away and taking a first former with her.'

'My goodness!' said Lucy, looking most astonished. 'That doesn't sound like Alice at all.'

'I don't understand why Jo – Alice – whatever you want to call her, would want to come back here,' said Pam. 'She didn't fit in, and no one liked her. It doesn't make sense.'

'It makes sense to me,' said Felicity, looking thoughtful. 'Bonnie, you were quite right when you said that Alice felt ashamed of herself and wanted to make amends. That is why she has come back to Malory Towers.'

'The locket!' cried Susan suddenly. 'Felicity, that locket

that we found, with the initials JJ engraved on it – I bet that it belonged to Alice!'

'Of course!' said Felicity. 'And it explains how she knew the end of Miss Grayling's speech – because she had heard it before, when she was in the second form!'

'Are you going to tell Miss Grayling?' asked Freddie, who had been listening open-mouthed. 'I shouldn't think that she would want a girl here who has already been expelled once.'

'I would be very surprised if Miss Grayling – and some of the other mistresses – don't already know who Alice is,' said Felicity. 'The Head must have agreed to take her back, and if she was willing to give her another chance I think that we should too.'

Most of the others agreed with this, though June wasn't convinced, saying in a hard voice, 'A leopard doesn't change its spots. As far as I am concerned, Jo has been putting on an act, trying to convince us that she is someone she isn't. Until we speak to her, and she explains her reasons for coming back to Malory Towers, I don't know whether I can trust her.'

'Are you going to tell her that we know her secret, Felicity?' asked Julie.

'Yes, for now that we know I think that it is better if we bring it all out into the open,' said Felicity. 'I will go and see her tomorrow.'

In the first-form dormitory, all was silent, for most of the girls were fast asleep. Only Violet was wide awake, for she meant to slip out of the dormitory shortly before midnight. The time seemed to creep by very slowly indeed, but at last it was ten minutes to twelve, and Violet got out of bed. It was a bitterly cold night, but the girl didn't want to get dressed, in case one of the others woke and saw her. So she put on her warm dressing-gown and outdoor shoes, placed the note that she had written to Faith on the girl's bedside cabinet, and slipped quietly from the room. A floorboard creaked as she tiptoed along the landing, and Violet stopped, her heart in her mouth. But no doors flew open and no mistress appeared on the scene, so the girl carried on down the stairs.

This is all very strange, she thought to herself. Here I am going out to rescue a cat – and perhaps meet a desperate kidnapper – dressed in my pyjamas!

A nervous giggle rose in her throat, but Violet quelled it, silently opening the big door that led into the garden. She shivered as a blast of cold air hit her, and suddenly realised that it was pitch black outside, with no moon to light her way.

'Why didn't I think to bring a torch with me?' thought Violet. 'Ah, I wonder if there is one in the cupboard!'

The big cupboard at the bottom of the stairs was home to all kinds of odds and ends, but there was no torch there. However, Violet did find an old-fashioned oil lantern and a box of matches. With a trembling hand, she struck a match and lit the wick, before stepping out into the cold and shutting the door softly behind her.

Violet felt very nervous indeed, trembling with cold and fear as she made her way to the big shed at the bottom of the garden. What if the kidnapper was inside, waiting for her? Oh, how she wished Faith was with her!

A sudden sound from inside the shed almost made her jump out of her skin, then she realised what it was. It was Willow mewing! Screwing up every ounce of courage she possessed, Violet pushed open the door, holding the lantern aloft as she peered inside. Relief made her go weak at the knees as she realised that there was no kidnapper there, only her own, beloved Willow. A rickety wood table stood in the middle of the shed, and Violet placed the lantern on it, before rushing to pick up Willow. The little cat had been rather cross with her mistress for neglecting her, but all that was forgotten now, and Willow purred in delight, rubbing her silky head against Violet's chin. As for Violet, she forgot that she was cold, forgot that she had been frightened, forgot *everything* except that she had found Willow!

'I had better get you back indoors,' said the girl at last. 'I shall have to carry you, so please don't wriggle!'

But Willow had decided that it was time to stretch her legs, and she suddenly jumped from Violet's arms, landing on the rickety table. The table wobbled dangerously, which Willow didn't like at all, and she leapt off at once, but the lantern that Violet had placed there fell to the floor, smashing and sending a sheet of flame across the dry wooden floor.

Snatching up Willow, Violet screamed, wondering if she dared run through the flames, which were between her and the door. But, even as she hesitated, the fire was spreading, the table alight now and flames shooting up the walls.

Violet coughed and choked, tears streaming down her cheeks, as she looked round desperately for a way out. But the only window in the shed was on the other side of the flames. She screamed again, as loudly as she could, praying that someone would hear her, but it was hopeless, for the thick, dark smoke was choking her. She was trapped, and no one was going to rescue her!

But Violet was wrong. Alice, feeling very restless from having slept so much during the day, simply couldn't sleep. Gingerly, for the girl still felt a little weak, she got out of bed and went across to the window. From her room she had an excellent view of the garden, and she started in fright as she spotted someone carrying a light darting across the lawn. Why, it was that first former, Violet! What mischief was she up to now? If she was caught out of her tower in the middle of the night, the girl would be in big trouble!

As a sixth former, it was up to Alice to see that she went back to bed, so the girl pulled on her dressing-gown and put on her slippers.

In the main San, one of the second formers was awake, and she whispered, 'Where are you going, Alice?'

'Never you mind,' said Alice. 'I shall be back shortly.'

The girl went quietly past the room where Matron slept and down the stairs, but as soon as she stepped outside, she smelled smoke.

'How odd!' she thought. 'It's a bit late for one of the gardeners to be having a bonfire. I wonder what it could be?'

As Alice came round the corner of North Tower, she was left in no doubt as to where the smell was coming from. The shed was ablaze! The shed that she had seen Violet enter a few minutes ago. Alice ran towards the fire, heart pounding and her mind racing. Was Violet still in there, or had she managed to get out? Then she heard a muffled scream, and knew the dreadful truth – Violet was trapped in the burning shed.

There was no time to raise the alarm or fetch help. Alice knew that she had to act quickly. Glancing round, she spotted a water butt nearby and, heedless of the cold, she pulled off her dressing-gown, soaking it in the water. Then, wrapping part of the dressing-gown round her hand, to protect it from the heat, she pulled open the shed door, the force of the blaze making her reel.

It was impossible to see anything because of the smoke and flames, and Alice called out, 'Violet, where are you?'

'Here!' croaked Violet. 'At the back of the shed.'

Then Alice did a very brave thing. She pulled her wet dressing-gown over her head, making sure that it covered as much of her as possible. And she ran through the flames to Violet.

The first former was sobbing with terror now, her face streaked with black, and she was still clutching Willow tightly. There was no time to enquire what the girl was doing with a cat, and Alice, with more courage than she felt, said, 'I'm going to get you out of here. Do exactly as I say, and don't hesitate. Now, put the cat in the front of your dressing-gown quickly!'

Violet did as she was told, then Alice put her own dressing-gown over both their heads, took Violet's arm in a firm grip, and shouted, 'RUN!'

The heat was almost unbearable as the two girls ran through the blaze, and Alice felt an agonising burning sensation to her hand. Their escape took only seconds, but to Violet and Alice it seemed like hours until they were outside, both of them collapsing on to the grass, coughing and choking.

Then there was a commotion, and the sound of raised voices, and Violet looked up to see Matron, Miss Grayling, two gardeners and several mistresses running towards them.

Matron had been woken by one of the second formers having a coughing fit, and had looked in on Alice only to find that she wasn't there. Then she had seen the blazing shed from the window, and raised the alarm.

'Good heavens!' she cried, as she saw the two girls lying on the ground, taking in their blackened faces and charred clothing. Then her sharp eyes spotted the burn on Alice's hand and she called out, 'Miss Grayling! We need to get Alice to hospital at once. She has a very bad burn and needs more expert treatment than I can give.'

'I shall telephone for an ambulance at once,' said the Head, going back into the school.

Miss Potts and Mam'zelle Dupont were also on the

scene and, as Matron carefully checked the two girls over, Mam'zelle stood wringing her hands, and moaning. Miss Potts was more practical, saying, 'Is there anything I can do to help, Matron?'

But, before Matron could answer, Mam'zelle suddenly spotted Willow, and cried, 'A cat! Why does Violet have a cat in her dressing-gown?'

Of course, Matron and Miss Potts had also noticed Willow, and Miss Potts said drily, 'We are all wondering that, Mam'zelle, but I am afraid that such questions will have to wait. The immediate need is to tend to the girls.'

Suddenly there came the wail of a siren, and everyone knew that the fire engine had arrived.

The two gardeners, who had been training hoses on the fire, stopped what they were doing, and went round to the front of the school to direct the fire engine.

Of course, the siren woke many of the girls up, and they looked out of the windows to see what was going on. They gasped when they saw the fire, and the people rushing about outside, most of them thinking that it was rather a thrill. Some of them made their way outside, not wanting to miss the excitement, and soon quite a crowd had gathered.

'Heavens, look at the old shed! It's been burnt to the ground!'

'Someone's been hurt! Look, it's Alice, of the sixth form.'

'And Violet! Goodness, I hope they aren't seriously injured.'

'Girls, do go back inside!' called out Miss Potts.

But, for once, no one took any notice of Miss Potts, and soon more girls came down, several of the first formers among them.

Daffy turned white when she took in the scene and saw the two girls lying on the ground, their faces black. And Willow was there too! For a moment she felt quite sick, but she simply had to find out what had happened, and whether Violet or Alice was badly hurt. So Daffy made her way across to where Miss Potts was bending over the girls, saying, 'Miss Potts, what happened?'

'As you can plainly see, Daphne, the shed caught fire,' said Miss Potts with sarcasm. 'How it caught fire is something we have yet to find out. Now, please get out of the way, for the ambulance will be here shortly.'

The ambulance arrived a few moments later, and everyone watched gravely as Alice was lifted on to a stretcher and put into the back. Violet had been lucky, as she had not suffered any burns at all, and did not need to go to hospital. But she had inhaled a large amount of smoke, and Matron took her to the San.

'Though that cat most certainly can't come,' she said sternly. 'Daffy Hope, make yourself useful and take it to the stables.'

'Yes, Matron,' said Daffy meekly, coming over and taking Willow from Violet.

'Oh, but she can't go to the stables!' Violet protested, her voice little more than a croak.

'Don't worry,' said Daffy in a very solemn whisper.

'I'll let Matron think that's where I'm taking Willow, but really I shall put her back in the box-room. And I shall take the greatest care of her, Violet, I promise.'

'Thanks, Daffy,' said Violet, rather surprised that Daffy was being so nice. It was probably just because she, Violet, had been in the fire and Daffy felt sorry for her. No doubt tomorrow, the girl would be back to her old, hostile self again!

With the two casualties gone and the fire almost out, there wasn't much left to see, and when Miss Potts again raised her voice and commanded that everyone go back to bed, she was obeyed.

Most of the girls were far too excited to sleep, though. Heavens, what a night it had been!

Daffy learns a lesson

The sixth formers hadn't heard the fire engine, as their dormitory was on the other side of North Tower, so they didn't hear the news until the following morning.

Mam'zelle Dupont, rather excited to be first with the news, stopped by the sixth-form table at breakfast, and told the girls of the dramatic events that had unfolded last night.

They listened in astonishment, and June said, 'Well! So Alice saved young Violet's life!'

'Ah, she is a heroine, that girl,' said Mam'zelle. 'The poor Violet was scarcely able to talk, but she managed to tell Matron that Alice ran through the flames to save her.'

'How brave of her!' said Susan. 'I'm not sure that I would have had that kind of courage.'

'Yes,' said June as Mam'zelle moved away. 'Anyone who shows the kind of bravery that Alice did last night has more than made amends for anything they did in the past. I wasn't sure about giving her another chance last night, but I jolly well am now! I vote that, when she comes back, we give Alice a hero's welcome.'

Everyone agreed at once, for all of them felt intensely proud of Alice.

'I wonder when she *will* be back,' said Bonnie. 'Mam'zelle said that she had burned her hand quite badly and, of course, she must have inhaled a great deal of smoke, just as Violet did.'

In fact, Alice returned to Malory Towers that very afternoon, but none of the sixth formers saw her, for Matron whisked her straight off to the San. The girl's hand had been bandaged, and she had a very sore throat, but she protested strongly.

'Matron, I feel quite well,' she said in a rather croaky voice. 'Really, I would far rather go back to the others.'

But Matron insisted, saying, 'You can join the others tomorrow, provided that you don't have a relapse. Come along now.'

And Alice, realising that it was quite useless to argue with Matron, followed her meekly.

Daffy, meanwhile, was in turmoil. Her conscience had kept her awake the night before, and she felt that she was to blame for everything that had happened. It was quite clear now that Violet must have found that note before she was meant to, and gone to the shed at midnight instead of midday. It was all because of her that Violet had been in the shed, and that Alice had been hurt. The first formers wondered why she was so subdued and unlike herself, but she refused to tell them. Katie guessed, of course, for she was also feeling very guilty at having gone along with Daffy's scheme.

'I wish that I had never let you talk me into it,' groaned Katie, for about the twentieth time that day as she and

Daffy walked through the courtyard after lunch.

'And I wish that I had listened to you,' said Daffy, sounding very miserable indeed. 'When I think what might have happened to Violet – and Willow – if Alice hadn't rescued her . . .' She broke off, giving a sudden sob, and Katie, who had never seen her friend cry before, realised how distressed she was.

'It's no good upsetting yourself,' she said rather awkwardly, giving Daffy a pat on the shoulder. 'Just be glad that Alice got there in time.'

'That's just it,' said Daffy, her voice almost breaking. 'I don't think that I shall ever feel glad about anything again until I get this off my conscience. I am going to own up to Miss Grayling.'

'Daffy!' gasped Katie. 'Are you sure?'

Daffy nodded firmly. 'I shan't mention your name, Katie, for you aren't to blame. You tried to talk me out of it, and I wouldn't listen.'

'Daffy, the Head is going to come down awfully hard on you,' said Katie, looking rather scared. 'She might even . . .'

The girl's voice tailed off, and Daffy said, 'Expel me? Yes, I know that.'

'But think how upset your people will be!' cried Katie.

Daffy's face quivered, but she took a deep breath, and said, 'The very last thing I want to do is hurt my parents. But I don't feel that I can stay at Malory Towers unless I own up, so either way I will have to leave.'

Katie understood this, and respected her friend for

making the difficult decision to tell Miss Grayling everything. All the same, she felt very unhappy as she watched her friend walk away, for the first form without Daffy just wouldn't be the same.

Miss Grayling had been to see Violet that morning and, although she had barely been able to croak, the girl had told her the whole story of how she had come to be in the shed, and how the fire had started.

When Violet had asked anxiously how she was to be punished, Miss Grayling had replied, 'Well, I think that what you suffered last night was punishment enough. And, as it is so close to the end of term, I shall allow you to keep your pet at school with you for the last few days. But please leave her at home next term, Violet, or I shall take a very dim view indeed!'

Violet, who had really feared that she might be expelled, felt most relieved, but the Head was far more worried than she had appeared, and later that day she sent for Miss Potts, to discuss the matter.

'I don't believe for a moment that the cat was taken by a kidnapper,' said Miss Grayling.

'I agree with you,' said Miss Potts. 'I think it is much more likely to have been one of the girls playing a trick.'

'Have you any idea who the culprit could be, Miss Potts?' asked the Head. 'After all, you know the first formers far better than I do.'

Miss Potts was just considering this when a knock came at the door.

Miss Grayling's voice was rather sharp as she called out,

'Come in!', for she was annoyed at being interrupted.

She frowned when Daffy Hope walked in, and said, 'Daphne, I am discussing something very important with Miss Potts at the moment, and must ask you to come back later.'

But Daffy was afraid that her courage might fail her if she went away, and she said, 'Please, Miss Grayling, I need to speak to you now. It is very important, for it is about the fire last night.'

Miss Grayling and Miss Potts exchanged glances, and the Head said, 'That is exactly what we have been talking about, so I suppose we had better hear what you have to say. Go on, Daphne.'

So, haltingly, with a great deal of prompting from the two mistresses, Daffy confessed to hiding Willow, and sending the note that had lured Violet to the shed last night. As she had promised, she kept Katie's name out of it and shouldered the whole blame herself. The Head and Miss Potts both looked extremely grave by the time she had finished, and Miss Grayling said heavily, 'You are very lucky, Daphne, that your prank did not end tragically.'

'I know that, Miss Grayling,' said Daffy, her voice trembling. 'That is why I had to get it off my conscience.'

'Well, that is to your credit, I suppose,' said the Head, looking very stern indeed. 'Though it doesn't alter the fact that you behaved very foolishly.'

Daffy hung her head, and Miss Potts asked, 'Daphne, why did you take Violet's cat?'

Daffy hesitated. She couldn't mention the feast, or all

of her form would be in trouble. So she said, 'I don't like her, Miss Potts. And I wanted to get back at her for something she had done to me.'

'I see,' said Miss Potts. 'So your motive was a desire for revenge.'

'Yes,' said Daffy, thinking that it sounded rather horrible when Miss Potts put it like that. 'I suppose it was.'

'Nothing good ever comes out of vengeance or vindictiveness,' said Miss Grayling. 'When a person is motivated by spite, someone always gets hurt. Sometimes it is the person who that spite is directed at, but often it hurts the person who is taking revenge just as badly. I trust that you have learned that, Daphne.'

'I have, Miss Grayling, and it is a lesson that I will never forget,' said Daffy with feeling.

Miss Grayling did not doubt the girl's sincerity. She had received a huge shock, and had shown great courage in owning up. But what she had done was so serious that it could not go unpunished.

An uncomfortable silence stretched, as the Head considered what she should do with Daffy. At last, the girl could bear it no longer, and she blurted out, 'Are you going to expel me, Miss Grayling?'

'I am not going to make that decision,' said Miss Grayling. 'Violet and Alice are. They both need to rest today, so I shan't tell them about your confession until tomorrow. But your fate is in their hands. You may go now.'

Daffy went, feeling sick at heart. She remembered the

time she had pulled Violet into the swimming-pool, and Alice had accidentally fallen in, too. The two of them were sure to want her expelled, and the girl couldn't find it in her heart to blame them!

Alice, meanwhile, was delighted to receive a visit from Felicity, who arrived bearing an enormous bouquet of flowers, which the whole of the sixth form had clubbed together to buy.

'How beautiful!' exclaimed Alice, thrilled. 'I really don't deserve them.'

'You most certainly do,' said Felicity, arranging the flowers in a vase that Matron had given her. 'You're a real heroine.'

'Nonsense,' said Alice gruffly, turning red. 'Anyone would have done what I did.'

'I'm not so sure,' said Felicity. 'Anyway, the point is, anyone *didn't* do it, you did, and we are all very proud of you.'

'How is Violet?' asked Alice, who was back in her little room and hadn't seen the girl since last night. 'And Willow, of course?'

'Both fine,' said Felicity. 'Violet escaped without any burns, though she has a very sore throat from all the smoke. As for Willow, Miss Grayling has allowed her to stay for the rest of the term, and she's having the time of her life being thoroughly spoilt by absolutely everyone!'

Alice laughed at this, which brought on a fit of coughing, and Felicity patted her on the back, saying, 'Poor thing! How is your hand?'

'Sore!' said Alice. 'But the doctor said it should heal nicely in time.'

Alice was so pleased to have company that she seemed to have lost some of her shyness, and chattered away. And, as Felicity listened, she could hear traces of Jo Jones coming through. Jo had been a dreadful chatterbox, bumptious, boastful and conceited. No one could call Alice bumptious, boastful or conceited, but she was gaining confidence, and that, thought Felicity, was a very good thing. She had made up her mind not to tell Alice that the sixth form knew her true identity just yet, for the girl had enough to deal with at the moment. But, in the end, Alice gave herself away.

The two girls were talking about June, and how great a success she had been as games captain. Alice, feeling more relaxed than she had since she started at Malory Towers, forgot to guard her tongue, and said, 'Who would have thought it? I remember her so well as a bold, mischievous second former . . .'

Then Alice's voice died away as she realised what she had said, and she turned pale. And Felicity knew that this was the time to bring Alice's secret out into the open.

'It's all right, Jo,' she said. 'We know who you are. By the way, which should I call you – Alice or Jo?'

Alice turned even paler, hardly able to speak for a moment, but at last she said in a strangled voice, 'Alice.'

'Very well,' said Felicity pleasantly. 'Alice it is.'

'How long have you known?' asked Alice, her voice

hardly more than a whisper, and her eyes wide behind the glasses.

'Only since yesterday,' said Felicity. 'Though you've had us puzzled for quite a while.'

She went on to tell the girl about the photograph she had seen in Matron's room, then asked, 'Why did you come back to Malory Towers, Alice? And why the change of name?'

Alice was silent for a moment, then she began quietly, 'I went to several schools after Malory Towers, you know. And at each one, I realised more and more what a splendid school this was, and what a marvellous opportunity I had wasted. And I began looking at my own behaviour, and realising why I didn't fit in here, and why people disliked me so. I decided that I didn't want to be Jo Jones any more, that I wanted to change myself completely.'

'Heavens!' said Felicity, listening to this in amazement. 'And how did your parents react to that?'

Felicity remembered the girl's parents well, especially Mr Jones, who had been every bit as loud and bumptious as Jo herself!

'Father didn't like it, of course,' said Alice. 'He liked me as I was, for I was just like him. And when I decided that I didn't want to be like him any more, he thought that it meant I was ashamed of him.' The girl took a deep breath, and said, 'Well, I *was* ashamed of him in many ways. You know what he was like, Felicity, always pushing himself forward and airing his opinions, and not showing any respect for people's feelings. I couldn't see it when I was younger, but I do now. Of course, I still love him dearly,' she added. 'I just wanted him to learn to be a little less full of himself, and more considerate of other people, as I was trying to be.'

'Well, you have succeeded very well indeed,' said Felicity. 'But what about your father?'

'He really has improved a lot,' said Alice with a smile. 'Remember I told you that he helped me to study for School Cert by asking me questions? Well, that was true. A few years before, he would have told me not to waste my time studying, for *he* never did. That just shows how much he has changed.'

'It certainly does!' said Felicity, astonished. 'Alice, how did you get Miss Grayling to agree to give you another chance at Malory Towers?'

'I telephoned her myself,' said Alice. 'I knew that it was no use asking Father to do it, for although he has changed a lot, he can still be tactless at times. Miss Grayling listened to what I had to say, though, and knew that I was sincere. So she agreed that I could join the sixth form at Malory Towers. Of course, she knew how unpopular I had been with you others, so she agreed to me using my middle name, Alice, and my mother's maiden name.'

'You have changed your appearance, too,' said Felicity. 'You were fair when you were in the second form.'

'Yes,' said Alice, flushing a little. 'That wasn't my real colour, though. I used to dye it! Shocking, wasn't it?'

'Shocking!' agreed Felicity with a laugh. 'And you have lost an awful lot of weight, too.'

'Yes, I was a tubby little thing in those days,' said Alice, grimacing. 'I feel much healthier now.'

Felicity looked hard at Alice for a few moments, then she asked suddenly, 'Are you happy, Alice?'

'I am happier than I was when I was cocky, conceited Jo,' answered the girl, after considering this for a minute. 'But I'm not *completely* happy, for I feel that I don't know who I really am. You see, Felicity, Jo wasn't the real me – although I thought she was at the time. But really, I was just acting the way that my father wanted me to act, trying to please him. Do you understand?'

'I think so,' said Felicity. 'But what about Alice? Isn't she the real you, either?'

'Parts of her are,' answered the girl. 'But, inside, I am not really as meek and timid as I have made out.'

'I can tell you one thing that is real,' said Felicity. 'And that is your bravery last night. You can't possibly pretend to have courage like that.'

'To be honest, I didn't know I had it in me to act like that,' said Alice. 'But once I knew that Violet was in danger, I didn't even stop and think that I might be hurt.'

'You probably have all sorts of hidden qualities, if only you will be yourself, and let them come to the fore,' said Felicity. 'I think that is what you should do, Alice – just be yourself.'

Alice felt as if a weight had rolled off her shoulders after her talk with Felicity. She hadn't felt comfortable about hiding her identity from the others, although she had done it with the best of motives.

Felicity had assured her that the others didn't think any the worse of her for her deception, adding honestly, 'June wasn't too sure at first, but your courage in saving Violet convinced her that you deserve to be given a chance. Everyone thinks you're a proper heroine.'

The girl felt warmed by these words, and found that she couldn't wait to get back to the sixth form tomorrow. And she was going to take Felicity's advice, and be herself!

Before she joined the others in class the next morning, Alice was surprised to be summoned to the Head's room.

Miss Grayling greeted her with a charming smile and said, 'How are you feeling today, Alice?'

'Much better, thank you, Miss Grayling,' answered the girl.

'I am pleased to hear it,' said the Head. 'My dear, your courage the other night averted a great tragedy, and I am very proud of you indeed.'

Alice, feeling as though she might burst with pride, turned very red, and stammered out a thank you.

'And now I am going to ask you to do something else, which requires a different kind of courage,' said Miss Grayling. 'I think that it is time for you to tell the others who you really are.'

'Oh, but they already know, Miss Grayling,' said Alice. 'Felicity came to see me yesterday, and she told me that – thanks to an old photograph in Matron's room – the girls had discovered my true identity.'

'Well,' said Miss Grayling. 'I always knew that the

sixth formers were very shrewd. They are very kind-hearted and just, too, generally speaking.'

'Felicity has already assured me that I will be welcomed back with open arms,' said Alice, smiling at the Head.

'I am glad to hear it,' said Miss Grayling, smiling back at the girl. 'But before I let you join them, I need you to make a decision, Alice. It won't be an easy one, for someone else's future rests on it.'

Alice looked very puzzled indeed, and rather alarmed, but before the Head could enlighten her, a knock came at the door and Miss Potts entered, followed by Violet and Daffy.

Violet looked just as puzzled as Alice felt, while Daffy looked very subdued and unhappy. The girl's eyes looked suspiciously red, as if she had been crying. But surely not, thought Alice. What could the happy, carefree Daffy have to cry about?

Miss Potts left to go back to her class, and Miss Grayling said seriously, 'Alice and Violet, Daphne has something to say to you both, and when she has finished I want you both to make a decision. That decision will be whether or not Daphne remains at Malory Towers.'

A marvellous end to the term

Unable to meet the eyes of the two girls, Daffy confessed to them, as she had confessed to Miss Grayling the day before.

Violet could not contain herself when she learned that it was Daffy who had taken Willow, and burst out, 'You mean beast! You knew how worried and upset I was. You could have put me out of my misery in an instant, but you didn't.'

'I'm sorry,' said Daffy, looking Violet in the eye for the first time. 'If I could only turn back the clock, I would. I have never felt so dreadful in my life as when I knew that the shed had caught fire, and that you and Alice had been hurt. And I hope that I never feel like that again. I've learned my lesson, but I shan't blame either of you if you want me expelled. I should probably feel the same if I was in your shoes.'

Miss Grayling, who had listened in silence, never taking her eyes off Daffy, turned to Alice and Violet now, saying, 'Well, girls?'

There was a moment's silence, then Alice said, 'Miss Grayling, when I was not very much older than Daffy, I was sent away from Malory Towers in disgrace. Only after I had left did I realise what a splendid school it is.'

Of course, this was news to the two first formers, who stared at Alice open-mouthed.

'I was lucky enough to be given a second chance,' the girl went on. 'Though I had to wait several years for it. So I am certainly not going to deny Daffy *her* second chance. I vote that she should stay at Malory Towers, and sincerely hope that she will come to realise what a marvellous school it is, as I did. And I also hope, Daffy, that – if you stay – you take the opportunity to show that you are truly sorry, and to do better in the future.'

Daffy felt a small – a very small – glimmer of hope. It was all up to Violet now.

The girl had listened intently to what Alice said, and now she turned to Daffy, as she began, 'Daffy, I think that what you did was low and mean and nasty,' she said. 'But, while I've been lying in the San, I have had time to think about my own behaviour. And I have come to realise that I can be a boastful, conceited little beast at times.'

Daffy gasped, while Miss Grayling and Alice exchanged an amused glance at Violet's frankness.

'I can understand why you wanted to take me down a peg or two,' went on Violet. 'Though the way that you went about it was quite wrong. But I am in no position to judge you, and I agree with Alice. I think that you should be given another chance at Malory Towers.'

'Thank you, girls,' said Miss Grayling. 'Daphne, I echo the words of Alice and Violet. You have been very lucky indeed, for few people are given the chance to start afresh. Make the most of it.'

'I shall,' said Daffy fervently, feeling quite weak with relief. She really had thought that she was going to be expelled, and the thought of leaving Malory Towers, and of her parents' pain and disappointment, had weighed heavily on her. 'Thank you, Miss Grayling. And as for you, Alice, and you, Violet . . . well, I can't find the words to tell you how grateful I am to both of you. I do realise what a fine school Malory Towers is, and I mean to make myself worthy of my place here. I shall own up to the others, of course, and I daresay they will send me to Coventry, for a bit, but –'

'Daphne, that isn't necessary,' interrupted Miss Grayling in a firm tone. 'You have owned up to the two people who were affected by what you did, and they have forgiven you. I see no reason for you to make your fresh start here difficult by setting the first formers against you.'

'Miss Grayling is quite right,' said Violet, as Daffy turned this over in her mind. 'I shan't tell any of the others, you may be sure of that.'

'Nor shall I,' said Alice.

'Then the matter is settled,' said Miss Grayling. 'There is no more to be said. You may go.'

'Miss Grayling, there is something else I would like to say, if I may,' said Violet. Miss Grayling nodded, and Violet turned to Alice.

'I haven't had a chance to thank you yet, for what you

did the other night,' she said. 'You risked your life to save mine and Willow's. Just saying *thank you* doesn't seem enough somehow.'

'It's more than enough,' said Alice, giving the girl a pat on the shoulder. 'And now, I rather think that Miss Grayling would like to have her study to herself.'

The Head fell into a reflective mood after the three girls had left. It had been a dramatic term, but, on the whole, a good one, she thought. Felicity Rivers had done a first-rate job as Head Girl, but then, Miss Grayling had never doubted that she would. And Alice – or Jo, as she had once been – had proved that she was a very worthwhile person indeed, with more in her than the Head had ever suspected.

The first formers had been very troublesome this term, but it looked as if Violet was beginning to see the error of her ways, and Miss Grayling hoped that it would help her to change them. According to Miss Potts, Faith, too, was changing, beginning to show signs of leadership, and the others were starting to respect her. The Head was very pleased, for this would stand Faith in good stead in the future. As for Daphne Hope – the girl had a lot of good qualities, and could do well for herself and the school. But she also had a lot of faults, and would have to strive to make the good cancel out the bad. She was a strong character, though, and Miss Grayling knew that – with a little guidance – she could do it. On the whole, decided the Head, things had worked out very well indeed.

The last week of term was a full one. Alice returned to

class after her visit to the Head's room and was given three rousing cheers by the proud sixth formers. Even the serious Miss Oakes beamed at the girl and patted her on the back.

Alice was the heroine of the school, for everywhere she went, girls and mistresses wanted to cheer her, or shake her good hand, and tell her how they admired her bravery.

'Heavens, I shall get a swollen head if this goes on for much longer,' said Alice, quite red-faced.

'No, *Jo* would have got a swollen head,' said June, clapping the girl on the shoulder. 'But *Alice* is far too decent a person.'

June hadn't been in the best of moods for the last few days, for she still hadn't solved the problem of how to replace those members of her lacrosse teams who had gone down with the flu – and the matches were to be played the day before term ended. Now, though, she had finally got to grips with things, and made some decisions.

At break-time she approached Felicity and Susan, and said, 'I have some news for you. You are both playing in the upper-school match against Marlowe Hall on Thursday.'

The two girls stared at June, quite speechless. At last, Felicity found her voice, and said, 'But, June, we have hardly played at all this term, because of the exams and our extra duties. What if we let you down?'

'As long as you try your best you won't let me down,'

223

said June. 'And I know that you will both do that. Can I count on you?'

The girls knew that June had been having difficulty making up her teams, and that if they didn't play, the match might have to be cancelled. That, of course, was quite unthinkable, and, with the honour of Malory Towers at stake, both of them chorused, 'Yes!'

'We shall have to spend the next couple of days practising like mad,' said Susan.

'Well, what are you waiting for?' laughed June. 'You are both free now until after lunch, so off you go to the lacrosse field!'

June then went in search of Daffy, and found her in the courtyard, chatting with Katie, Faith and Violet.

'Daffy!' she called. 'I want to see you at the lower-school lacrosse practice this afternoon.'

'Of course, June,' said Daffy, who had vowed to be on her very best behaviour from now on. 'I'll be there all right.'

'Good,' said June, 'because you are in the team against Marlowe Hall on Thursday.'

For a moment, Daffy thought that she hadn't heard June properly, then Katie gave a whoop of joy and thumped her on the back. 'Good show, Daffy! We shall be playing together. Isn't that marvellous?'

'I'll say,' said Daffy, her voice quivering with excitement. 'Thank you, June. I shall shoot *dozens* of goals, you see if I don't!'

As June walked away, Faith congratulated Daffy too,

but Violet said nothing. And Daffy, who felt that a new understanding had sprung up between the two of them, felt rather hurt.

Then Violet gave a haughty sniff and said, 'Of course, you know that June only chose you because so many of the others are ill, don't you?'

Daffy whipped round to stare at the girl, hardly able to believe her ears, then she saw that Violet was grinning.

'Only joking, old girl!' she laughed, giving Daffy a playful punch on the arm. 'I'm simply thrilled for you!'

Then Daffy laughed too, while Katie and Faith exchanged startled looks. Heavens, only the other day Violet and Daffy had been bitter enemies, and now they were on their way to being the best of friends! Whatever next?

Felicity, Susan and Daffy stuck to their word, all three of them spending every spare minute on the lacrosse field over the next few days. Then it was Thursday, and the teams climbed aboard the big coach that was to take them to Marlowe Hall.

The lower school played first, while the upper school watched and cheered them on.

'Daffy's going to have her work cut out,' said Felicity. 'The girl marking her is twice her size.'

'Yes, but Daffy is very agile and very fast,' said June. 'I don't think that her opponent will be able to keep up with her.'

And June was quite right, for as soon as Daffy got the ball into her net, she was off down the field like a streak of lightning, before passing to Katie, who was very near the goal. Katie aimed for the goal, but just missed, causing the watching Malory Towers girls to groan.

'Bad luck, Katie!' called out Susan.

The two teams were very evenly matched, but a few minutes later one of the Marlowe Hall girls broke away from the girl marking her and shot a goal. Then, just before the whistle blew for half-time, Marlowe Hall scored again!

June was in despair, but although she groaned inwardly, she sportingly applauded the girl who had scored, for it really had been a most spectacular goal.

The lower-school team looked rather dispirited as they sank down on to the grass to rest, and June ran on to the field.

'Cheer up!' she said. 'You're all doing splendidly and you mustn't lose heart. There is still a long way to go before the match is over.'

Her words put new heart into the girls, and they started the second half full of fighting spirit. And it paid off, for after only five minutes, Rita of the second form shot a goal. The team were inspired after that, and a little later Maggie also shot one.

Felicity and Susan hugged one another excitedly, while June cried, 'We're even! Come on, Malory Towers! Play up!'

And the girls did play up, putting every effort into stopping the Marlowe Hall girls from shooting any more goals.

Then, with only a few minutes of play left, Daffy found herself with the ball in her net and a clear shot at goal. The only trouble was, she was so far away that she wasn't certain if she could get the ball in. Rita, however, was closer, and if Daffy were to pass the ball to her, she was almost certain to score. Daffy hesitated for a moment. How marvellous it would be if she were the one to shoot the winning goal! And wouldn't it be something to tell the others when she returned to Malory Towers. But what if she missed? There would be no glory in that! Besides, if she passed to Rita, she would still have played a big part in scoring the goal. All of these thoughts ran through Daffy's head in an instant and, in that instant, Daffy got an inkling of what team spirit was all about. The ball flew from her net to Rita's, the second former caught it and flung it towards the goal, and then a great cheer went up, just as the whistle blew.

They had won! Malory Towers had won!

The upper-school team yelled themselves hoarse, thumping one another on the back, until June cried, 'I say! We had better go and get changed, for our match starts shortly. Come along, everyone!'

Then it was the turn of the lower school to cheer on the older girls, which they did with great enthusiasm.

'Good show, June!'

'Come on, Felicity!'

'Oh, rotten luck, Susan!'

Once again, the match was a very close and exciting one. Neither Felicity nor Susan shot a goal, though they tried their hardest, but June did, and won the match for her team.

As June shook hands with the captain of the opposing team, the younger girls jumped up and down, hugging one another in excitement.

And no one was more thrilled than Daffy, who felt as if she might burst from happiness. It just goes to show, she thought. There are other ways of having fun besides fooling around and playing jokes. All the same, I expect I *shall* get up to mischief occasionally, for it's in my nature. But, from now on, I shall think things through properly before I play a trick, and make sure that no one can be hurt, for there is nothing funny in that at all!

Daffy thought that the day couldn't get any better, but she was wrong, for June came and sat down beside her on the coach back to Malory Towers, and said, 'Well done, Daffy. You played jolly well today.'

Daffy turned red with pleasure, and said, 'Thanks, but I didn't do anything marvellous. Why, I didn't even shoot a goal.'

'No, but you made it possible for Rita to shoot one, and win the match for us,' said June. 'I was watching you, and saw you hesitate, wondering if you should try and aim for goal yourself.'

Daffy looked at June in surprise, wondering how on earth the games captain could have known what had been going through her mind.

June laughed, and said, 'I know exactly what you were thinking, because the same thoughts would have gone through my mind when I was your age. In fact, I was once in your position, but I decided to try and grab the glory for myself, and shot for goal.'

'What happened?' asked Daffy, her eyes wide.

'I missed,' said June ruefully. 'And our team lost the match. So you see, Daffy, you made the right decision. You have a lot more team spirit than I did when I was a youngster, and are a great deal more sensible.'

Sensible! What a horrid word, thought Daffy. She had made up her mind to turn over a new leaf, but she didn't want to go too far and become all sensible and dull and goody-goody. That would never do! What a pity that it was the end of term tomorrow and there wasn't time to plan another trick on Mam'zelle. Well, she would come back next term with plenty of tricks up her sleeve, and show everyone that, although the new Daffy was kind and thoughtful, she still knew how to make people laugh!

'Well, this has rounded off the term nicely,' said Felicity cheerily as the lacrosse teams arrived back at Malory Towers tired, untidy, hungry – and very, very happy.

'I should say,' agreed Susan. 'My word, I'm starving! Hope there's something good for supper.'

'There's sure to be, as it's the last night,' said June. 'Come on, there's just time to tidy ourselves up a bit and get changed before the bell goes.'

Of course, word had got round that both teams had won their lacrosse matches, and the players were absolutely thrilled when they entered the dining-room, and everyone got to their feet to applaud them.

'Very well done, girls,' called out Miss Potts. 'We are extremely proud of you all.'

Then everyone took their seats and tucked in for, as June had predicted, it was a most delicious supper.

There were fat, juicy sausages and fluffy mashed potatoes, all smothered in gravy, followed by treacle pudding with custard. And, if anyone was still hungry after that, they could help themselves to cheese and biscuits.

Everyone ate hungrily, and Felicity noticed that even Alice, who normally had a poor appetite, seemed to be enjoying the meal.

The girl seemed much more relaxed and less timid now that her secret was out, and Felicity was pleased to see her chattering happily to Nora as she ate.

'I say, Alice!' she called out. 'Will you be coming back to Malory Towers next term?'

'Yes,' said the girl, looking pleased. 'If things had gone badly for me this term, I probably wouldn't have, but as it is you've all been awfully decent to me.'

The others were pleased to hear this, for they had grown to admire Alice enormously, both for her ability to see her faults and change them, and for her courage.

'It's been a funny old term,' said Felicity. 'What with all the mystery surrounding Alice, and the trouble that the first formers have caused. As for Daffy Hope, I simply can't believe how mistaken I was in her character!'

'Well, you can hardly be blamed for that,' said Susan. 'Even her parents don't realise how naughty she is!

She had most of the mistresses fooled at first, too, with her innocent act, though Miss Potts saw through her fairly quickly.'

'She's not a bad kid at heart, though,' said Felicity, looking across at the first-form table, where Daffy was chattering nineteen to the dozen with her friends. 'And I shall certainly keep an eye on her next term!'

Many of the girls found it hard to sleep that night, for they were all excited at the thought of going home for the Christmas holidays. Even Felicity, quite worn out from her strenuous lacrosse match, found her mind racing as she thought of what fun it would be to spend Christmas with her parents and Darrell. At last, though, she dropped off, and didn't stir until the bell rang the following morning.

Even Nora, who normally hated getting out of bed, was up on time, for she was as excited about going home as anyone.

After breakfast, there was the usual last-minute panic as everyone packed their trunks and hunted for long-lost items.

'Oh, *where* is my hairbrush?'

'Pam, have you seen my slippers?'

'Lucy, why you are packing a photograph of *my* parents in *your* trunk, I don't know!'

Things were even more chaotic in the first-form dormitory, for Willow had been brought down from the box-room and thought that it was great fun to climb in and out of the open trunks.

'One of us is going to end up taking her home, if you don't keep an eye on her, Violet,' said Katie.

'No chance of that,' laughed Violet. 'I'm not going to risk losing her again.'

Daffy flushed a little at this, for she always felt uncomfortable when reminded of the time that she had taken Willow and, seeing this, Violet quickly changed the subject, saying, 'My goodness, won't it be fun to be at home for Christmas?'

Daffy threw the girl a grateful look. Violet really had changed a lot just lately, she thought, and had become a much nicer person.

At last it was time for the girls to gather in the hall. Some of them were being collected by their parents, while others were waiting for the coaches that would take them to the railway station.

Susan's parents were coming to drive her and Felicity home, and as the two girls waited patiently, Susan said, 'Heavens, what a din! And most of it caused by the first formers!'

'Well, we were just like them once,' said Felicity with a grin. 'And, one day, they will be just like us!'

'Only two more terms,' said Susan rather wistfully. 'And then we leave Malory Towers for good.'

'Yes, but we must try not to feel sad about it,' said Felicity, giving her friend's arm a squeeze. 'Otherwise it will spoil the time that we have left.'

'Yes, you're quite right,' said Susan, glancing out of the window. 'Oh good, Mother and Father are here.

Got your things, Felicity? Come along then.'

And, calling 'goodbye' to the others, the two girls walked out of the school, Felicity wondering what was in store for her during her final two terms at Malory Towers.

Plenty of fun, I expect, as well as some shocks and surprises. We shall have to come back and see!

EGMONT PRESS: ETHICAL PUBLISHING

Egmont Press is about turning writers into successful authors and children into passionate readers – producing books that enrich and entertain. As a responsible children's publisher, we go even further, considering the world in which our consumers are growing up.

Safety First
Naturally, all of our books meet legal safety requirements. But we go further than this; every book with play value is tested to the highest standards – if it fails, it's back to the drawing-board.

Made Fairly
We are working to ensure that the workers involved in our supply chain – the people that make our books – are treated with fairness and respect.

Responsible Forestry
We are committed to ensuring all our papers come from environmentally and socially responsible forest sources.

**For more information, please visit our website at
www.egmont.co.uk/ethical**